Unvisited Spaces

and twelve other stories

ALSO BY F. E. MAZUR

Spine

The Buckseller

The Halftone Man

No Applause for Franush

visited paces

and twelve other stories

F. E. Mazur

Royalty Ridge
Springfield, Kentucky
2014

FIRST PRINT EDITION

A Kindle Edition was made available to readers in 2011.

Address for Correspondence:
ROYALTY RIDGE BOOKS
1610 Royalty Ridge
40078

ISBN-13   978-0692200926
ISBN-10   0692200924

Contents

bUSEs

My friend Chance called me one morning while it was still dark out. He wanted to get hold of me before I was off to work. He was living in New York where, a year ago, he'd gone to be an actor. He shared a loft with a writer and a painter, but one was heading to Europe for a couple of months and the other to China.

"Take some time off and drive up," he said. "Think about the Fourth. You've never been to the Big Apple, right? We'll put away a few beers, and I'll show you the sights. I know some women, too."

The women sounded good because I hadn't been with the opposite sex for a while, and a measure of inferiority was becoming the real prick in my morning routine. But driving there, I didn't know about that.

"I heard you have to pay to get into the city," I said.

"Better than having to pay to get out," he said.

I hadn't had my coffee yet and couldn't tell what exactly he meant or if he was kidding around, but I'd already been down on my luck once in my early life when there wasn't enough money to buy a quart of milk, and I didn't know how a person could steal his way out of a city.

"I'm not used to driving in big cities," I said.

"So take a bus. We'll meet at Port Authority and catch a cab from there to my place. Don't think about it. Just do it."

For some reason, the bus idea intrigued me. I suppose it was because I'd never been on one, except for a school bus that had hauled my ass and trumpet around to football games and whose road rhythm often threatened a wet explosion down below. But the big cruisers, the kind that carried people all over the country, those I'd not set foot on.

I'd look at them, though. Every time one was near, including those that barreled past me on the highway, I couldn't help but glance up at it and try to see the people inside. There was something about their sitting high above me, like they had been selected to go to a special place, and their elevation and the speed of the bus seemed to prove it.

Nighttime was when the big things really fascinated me. You could see through the tinted glass easier than in the daytime because some of the riders would have a light on overhead if they were reading or doing something with their hands, and the bus and its people appeared like a miniature world all to itself. Once, while I stood on a corner waiting to cross, a Greyhound pulled up and behind the window to the side of me was a young woman, her face soft and smooth like fresh snow on a moonlit hilltop. She had her light on above, even though she was staring at nothing and not doing anything from what I could tell. It was a perfectly peaceful scene, even with the lazy rumble from the diesel, and this beautiful creature appeared bummed, to say the least. I was standing in darkness, I knew this, but I raised a hand anyhow and waved. She saw me despite the darkness. And tilting her head forward, much like the Madonnas I'd stared at when growing up as an obedient Catholic kid, she smiled ever so faintly. I'd wished then and there I could be traveling on that bus to wherever it was going.

*

The day I left for New York was the same day a local woman was reported killed in Iraq. It was a sunny Friday. The temps were in the 80s. The bus station uptown was a busy place because of the higher gas prices brought on by the war and the widening economic jaws of the Chinese, but also because the Greyhounds and Trailways shared the space with community transit. These local buses were always bellyaching about operating expenses. The threat surfaced every year they would discontinue service. Their latest effort to ward off bankruptcy, besides the new, creatively frugal catchphrase "bUSEs," was the selling off of the vehicle exterior, side and rear windows included, to a single advertiser.

As I waited on my ride to pull in from Springfield, one of these painted blocks on rolling rubber swung into a slot nearby, so

I got a good look. A radio station that switched its fare to Christian Rock and upped its wattage had control of its decoration. Gigantic brown crosses started above the rear wheels and stretched across the windows onto the roof, with the FM number and call letters above and below. There was also the station's new biblical sounding slogan wrapped around the cowling under the headlights. The background color bumper-to-bumper and top-to-bottom was a putrid green. It was an ugly bus, in my opinion. And with the painted-over windows, you couldn't tell who or what was on board. Oh, I know that if you were a rider you could see out, but what if you spotted someone on the sidewalk or coming out of a store that you wanted to wink or throw a kiss at? Or maybe you wanted to flip the bird. What would be the sense? During moments when I questioned my fellow countrymen and the condition of their hearts, I thought these buses with their painted one-way windows were just the vehicles that might have the people over in The King's Enclave someday saying to each other, *"Have you noticed? The homeless problem is no more."* Never wondering who was on those buses and where their passengers were being taken.

*

Earlier in the week, when I'd purchased my ticket, the woman behind the counter asked when I would want to leave. She had a thousand lines in her face and looked like she'd been working in the terminal for all of her life and maybe the previous one, too. She was cheerful nonetheless and said there were several daily runs to New York City that arrived from various points south and west. She rattled off the departure times. I chose the 4:15.

"You sure that's the one?" she asked. "It's not an express. It stops at a dozen small towns and, let's see … you won't arrive in New York until 7:10 the next morning."

Well, that's what I wanted. I wanted to experience riding the bus both when the sun was up and when it was not. I'd heard, too, that many passengers stepped off for the night and got themselves a motel room, so that you might even have a bus all to yourself.

9

But that wouldn't be the case with this ride. Nearing midnight, there were about ten of us trying to get comfy so that we might crash and not wake up with a crick in the neck and shoulders.

One passenger staying on was a girl who talked like she was over eighteen, but I thought she was probably jailbait. She'd been sitting on the left side of the aisle three or four seats behind the driver, and around midnight she turned back to me—because my mouth wasn't hung open like the others, I guess—and asked if I wanted company. I answered "Sure" because although my lids were starting to weaken, she was damn good-looking, jailbait or not.

But she wasn't a flirt, I can say that. She just wasn't tired, had read enough of her book for the day, a biography of a woman doctor, she said; and there wasn't anything to gaze at through the windows, what with it being night. And it was a joy of hers—her word, "joy"—that she liked to meet new people.

She asked if I was traveling the entire way to New York and I said I was, and she said she wasn't. Then she asked why I was going and I told her, to visit a friend who's an actor.

"Do I know him? Have I heard of him?" she wanted to know.

"I doubt it," I said.

"Tell me his name. Or is it a woman? Except you did say 'actor'."

"His name's Chance."

"What's his first name?"

"That's it. It's his stage name, too. I don't know if he's changed his mind on that."

"Like Madonna," she said.

"He was named after a cow," I told her, and I got to laughing as I said this, because it was a fact about my friend that always did make me laugh.

"Go on," she said, and laughed too. "A cow? Those things we get our eggs from?"

I grinned at her sense of humor and said, "The very same. Ever hear of a show, *The Waltons?*"

10

"That's before I was born," she said. "But Richard Thomas, I know, was its star."

"Well, the Walton family had a pet cow and Chance was its name, and that's what his parents named him after."

She then wanted to know what productions Chance—my friend, not the cow—had appeared in and I had to tell her I didn't have the faintest. The three or four telephone calls we'd exchanged in setting up my visit, I'd not asked and he'd not volunteered. We were of the same mind that most people don't really give a shit about what others are up to, and so our greetings to one another went something like: *"How's it going?" "Not too bad. How's it going with you?" "You know. Hanging in there."*

The real truth, however, was we were good friends ever since we'd turned the tables on an armed robber while working as teens at a Hometown Pizza (I'd deliberately made a move to distract the tattooed mother, and Chance slammed his head with a frying pan), and we did have a genuine interest in what the other was doing. Only there wasn't always the immediate need to know that you get with those people who have their nose up someone's ass.

*

Early morning though it was, and a Saturday to boot, Port Authority was still a long way from looking like a crapped-out party when I got there, and it was the first thing I said to Chance, whose long hair resembled the rotting brush pile out behind my apartment: "Who knew there were so goddamn many buses in the world and they're all gathering in New York on the same day I come for a visit."

"You're a popular guy, Bud," he said.

I grabbed my bag and we went out to the street and climbed into a cab. The driver sported some greasy black hair and a beard. And where heavy beard was absent, there was the ol' five o'clock shadow and plenty of sweat, although the sweat was most likely because he'd been working through the night. He had a thick accent and I assumed he was from that part of the world that involved a lot of bloodletting and is always in today's unhappy news.

I got to wondering how New Yorkers saw their immigrants these days. Since 9/11, that is. Where Chance and I come from, when people spoke of New Yorkers, it was said they'll tolerate everyone and anything. It was said with a little blow of air at the end. If that were ever true, I couldn't imagine that it was true after the twin towers fell. And the fucked-up mess in Iraq was saying there's no end to the number of these people eager to kill themselves in order to kill others. Rest assured if I were throwing a goddamn shindig of any kind, I wouldn't be inviting any Muslim immigrants any time soon. Invite them just to show yourself off as fair, open-minded, and that you don't paint them all with the same brush? The risk—just my opinion—wouldn't be worth it. Doing business the old way where you had to see your kid actually smoking weed before accusing him; where you first got a few photographs of the old man slipping it to his secretary before filing the papers; where you gathered the facts before making the accusation is what I'm saying; that way, depending on the matter, could get you killed nowadays. Today's world requires a dude to act on his hunch and live with the result. Whatever it is.

*

The taxi ride to Chance's took about ten minutes, and going up in the elevator almost as long, it seemed. I kept expecting it to die between floors and was certain the cracked red emergency button on the operator's panel would not work, the phone neither.

The loft was on the fifth floor of an old, I presumed no-longer used warehouse. The whole neighborhood was basically warehouse after warehouse, and many of the upper floors of these were now rental lofts—if the trimmings on the windows were any indication—with all types of small shops at the bottom. The first time that I looked out to see what the view of the big city was that Chance had every night when he turned in and every morning when he got up, I saw the huge sliding door on the street floor of

12

one warehouse closing behind a black car; and in the shadows beyond the car was a bus with painted-over windows.

Later that day, Chance treated me at a really nice restaurant, and two women joined us. He'd kept the second part as a surprise. Mine's name was Serendipity (and I almost said "Go on" like that girl I'd met on the bus less than twenty-four hours earlier). Within a few minutes, it was clear Serendipity didn't think much of her date. And I wasn't thrilled either. All the same, I endured because I had a hunch we'd both been doing similar exercise in the morning and were dedicated to putting a stop to it, at least for a while.

But here's how the mutual hatred started. I asked where and how far the twin towers were from where we were sitting, and she threw her head back and directed this to Chance: "Just how many hogs are on his farm?"

Chance kind of laughed, and his date did laugh. Then she turned back to me. "You didn't hear about the airplanes, baby? The big jets that some Arab screwballs crashed into the towers on purpose? And then the towers fell down and took about three thousand of us with them?"

"My god, Ser, he knows about Ground Zero," Chance said.

And I said, "I misspoke."

She turned her head toward the entrance and let out one of those laughs that you were supposed to think wasn't intended to be heard. "What are you? A budding politician?"

"Ser works down at Wall Street," Chance said in a kind of explanation. "She makes indecent amounts of money."

"I pay indecent taxes, too," she said.

"Well, the homeland thanks you," I dared.

Which is when she cocked her head at an odd angle and stared at me a time before saying, "The little half-assed hamlet you're from, Bud, whatever it's name…is it receiving some of that money earmarked for Homeland Security?"

"What if it is?"

Chance, he chuckled because he knew where she was coming from, the same as I, and figured I was just stoking her fire to have some fun. But that wasn't the case. I could agree that the terrorists' most likely target would again be a big city like New York, L.A., or Chicago. But it wasn't out of my realm of possibilities they would strike small towns, really small towns, podunks, and strike them all at the same time. Maybe a dozen of them spread across the country. What a statement they would make if each of those towns reported on the same day a hundred dead. I thought, too, they wouldn't even have to trouble themselves with a suicide bomber. Fuck no, they could just leave the loaded truck or van on Main Street, sort of like McVeigh had, and book; and no one in those little rural burgs would be the wiser. The message to America would be: *"We can hit you anywhere!"*

*

It was a big space, the loft, but there weren't any interior walls, just a couple six-feet high dividers, which the painter had decorated with partially clothed men and women (I'm no art critic, but I thought they were nicely done), and so hooking up in such an environment was a new experience for me. But Serendipity made it easy. She had her tough side—no faking the evening before as she was giving me the what-for—but a soft core emerged in the night, and I realized she was terrified that another terrorist attack would come. At the collapse of the towers she had been only a few blocks away, and the dust and ash that quickly billowed through the surrounding streets, the same stuff that I had watched safely on television while finishing an early beer at Applebee's on my day off, engulfed her. She told me in the night there were many moments when the taste and smell of the dust came back and overwhelmed her to where she would stop whatever she was doing and cry.

After Ser and her friend left in the morning, I asked Chance over coffee if he was afraid of maybe a dirty bomb coming into Manhattan. I knew I had other questions also when, seconds later, I watched him get up from his chair and remove a gun, a snub-nosed revolver, from a leather bag and place it on the table. I say "other questions" because somehow I was certain the gun was not related to my first.

"Ever hear of a book called *Babi Yar?*" he asked. I hadn't. "It's another story of the Nazis rounding up and murdering Jews. This one in the Ukraine."

I waited as he stared at me.

"At the front of the book is a quote from a poet. *'Let no one forget. Let nothing be forgotten.'* What do we have? We have: *'We will never forget.'*"

I must have shaken my head.

"Bud, this is New York. Where there's Broadway. Where's there's the *New Yorker*. Where there's lived some of the best writers in the world. Where there are some of the most daring publishers. There's no poetry in *'We will never forget.'*"

I could see it bothered him more than just some ordinary irritation as he uttered the statement yet again.

"Something about it doesn't inspire confidence that we know what the hell we're doing," he said. "That's all."

I waited a while before switching to a different topic: "What's with the gun?"

"You can take it when you leave," he said without interest. "There's no inspection of bags on a bus, is there?"

"Is it real?"

"It's a cheapie, but it's real. There's even enough shells to load it."

He understood when I didn't reach out and pick up the gun.

"You don't want it?"

"I don't think so," I said.

"It's nothing to do with terrorism," he said, probably aware that I was wondering why he had the thing in the first place, since we each knew the other had no interest in firearms for hunting or protection.

It turned out he was to read for a part in an off-Broadway production and the character recited many of his lines with a gun in hand. He'd wanted the feel of what that was like. The part was bigger than anything he'd done to date, he really was hoping to land it, and when some of his theatrical friends refused to cop to owning a handgun that he could borrow, he took a chance and went out on the street to obtain one. While the gun most likely had been stolen to begin with, he eased his conscience of having it with the belief that he was possibly preventing a killing, simply because it was in his responsible possession and not some criminal's.

"How about you listen to me read," he said. "Tell me what you think."

"Hey, the last play I sat through was in high school," I told him. "And that was only because I had it bad for a girl with a role. I don't know fuck about acting."

"Then you're perfect," he said.

And so was he. Later, when he read for Ser and her friend, they agreed.

A gun is like cat shit, as it guarantees you'll take notice. Yet under the handling of Chance, the snub-nosed revolver was clearly a minor thing. Between when he grabbed it up and later set it back on the table, it seemed no more important than a coffee mug, or that frying pan. Even when the lines implied a threat to another character and required he raise and point the gun, it was out there in space like a new shoot on a tree limb. None of that tipping it to one side to show the wielder was a tough guy. I told him he was a cinch to get the part.

*

The Fourth of July brought an end to my four-day visit. It came more quickly than preferred since what Ser and I were doing, I liked a lot. Chance said he'd ride along with me in the cab to Port Authority, then walk back for a little exercise.

It was a bright day that was there for us and everyone in the city when we stepped out of the building onto the street, and the air had lost some of its unpleasantly civilized aroma. People were already appearing in numbers as most of them didn't have to work the holiday. As it was still the morning, many men and women

16

were sauntering in and out of the flag-decorated shops, especially the coffee shop and deli.

We checked up and down the street to see if a taxi was anywhere close that we could hail, but were out of luck. A second later a cheer went up behind us and as I swung around to look, to discover what it was about, it multiplied rapidly, joined by that Sousa fellow. Someone in a nearby apartment must have put on a CD of the composer's marches and stationed a speaker near an open window.

Encouraging the cheer was a bus, likely the same I'd had a glimpse of the day of my arrival. It had driven from the warehouse where there were no shops, and it was the most beautifully painted bus I'd ever seen, nothing commercial about it. All patriotism, it had a huge Old Glory billowing in two dimensions up and over the roof with wavy golden banners on the sides that read *God Bless America* and *We Will Never Forget*. Behind it was the black car that I'd seen at that same time, and it was now clean and so high gloss that it rivaled a soldier's spit-shine.

The bus turned left and the car went right, and each paused next to the curb. The driver of the spotless car got out, marched over to the warehouse door and rolled it shut. He signed to the bus driver before heading back to his vehicle. It drove off away from us, while the bus turned the corner onto our street and moved deliberately, as a number of other cars and delivery trucks were making their way. It was such a stunning and tastefully painted exterior to this bus that more people gathered on the sidewalks on both sides of the street, including guys from the deli who had on their white aprons and another guy from a tune-up shop who held an air hammer with the long compressed air hose still attached. Soon, people all along the sidewalks began to applaud, and it got louder and their cheering got louder, and a few started to whistle. Sousa, too, was cranked up, and I heard someone say the names of many of our soldiers killed in action in Iraq and Afghanistan were inscribed on the bus, and I thought of whoever was in charge of the paint job and marveled at his patience, since the bus would always

17

be a bus and not a monument, meaning someday it would end up in a junkyard. The whole scene grew into an event, and I couldn't imagine what was now happening in any other city, nor on a day other than the Nation's Day of Independence.

I myself got caught up in it. I started cheering, pumping my fist, hollering, and the Bud head swelled as I thought these city folk needed to be shown how to whistle. Dropping my bag, I slipped both pinkies into my mouth and blew like a sonovabitch. I took in just enough oxygen between blasts so there was hardly a break. Someone in the building behind was flinging out confetti, while the mechanic across the street raked the air with a series of raucous bursts from his hammer.

I turned to look at Chance, sure that he too was enjoying this unexpected grand start to the Fourth of July, only to find that he was bent over with his hands in my bag.

He was loading the gun. And there was a note beside it.

I can't say exactly what the mixture was racing through my head at that moment, except that he must have feared having an unlicensed gun in his possession for very long and that he had slipped the revolver and the shells into my bag while I was taking a final leak before we left his loft. I began to read the note as if it would clear my instant confusion, but he clicked the cylinder shut, inserted the gun behind his belt at the back and was off up the street in the direction of the bus, without a word.

I took two quick steps after him—maybe it was more, I can't say, and it's not important—before stopping myself cold.

And I prayed that he was right.

And I understood there was no choice but to accept that he was. The fellow would not be getting off. He would not walk a few blocks, then punch a number into his cellphone. He would stay in his seat is what he would do.

And I would have to stand where I was in order to avoid being the Devil's match.

And so I did. I watched my friend the actor approach the bus. Twenty feet away, he moved into the middle of the street. He raised his left hand and I could see the driver scowl and wave at him to get out of the way. In response, Chance raised the other hand and together they patted the air between the bus and himself as if to say, *"Calm down, I just have a question."*

The bus drew near and the driver put his face closer to the front window and gestured his thumb upward at the route display that read "Out of Service," and Chance patted the air harder without retreating or moving to either side. Finally, like that Chinese tank everyone's seen, the bus came to a stop rather than run over the person before it. Which is when I wondered if Chance had thought it through. All the way through. Did he realize not just what he had to do, but how it had to be done and how horrible the act would be? How he had to make as certain as possible that the arms, hands, the fingers especially, wouldn't move afterwards.

He stepped quickly then to the side of the bus and the driver opened the door for him. I could see Chance's eyes now. They held an actor's smile as the right hand found the gun. He brought the revolver around front and, at point-blank range, shot the bus driver in the face.

*

Louella. Her last name of African origin. Swahili, someone once said. Too many letters and too many unfamiliar combinations. In the end it was just Louella to all of us who knew her. Everyone had murdered it, even the local anchors. She'd been first a waitress, then a private, then dead. Dead by an IED.

As the cops swarmed, I'd spotted her name on the bus. It had been painted just to the left of the door. I thought she'd be grateful to Chance that it wasn't murdered yet again by a giant box of explosives.

That Fourth of July I caught a much later bus home. An express. It stuck to the interstates. Once the sun disappeared, the many small towns along the route began to set off their fireworks. The bursts were distant and so did not appear to be very far above the horizon. Everyone on the bus stared while each firework exploded without a sound. I stared too while I worried for America. I worried for Chance as well, even though he'd likely be getting all the dramatic parts he wanted. At least for a while.

OPERCULUM

Basteen wouldn't arrive at his cottage till two in the morning, and the lake was crashing. In the car's headlights he saw a familiar story: he'd paid good money for less than competent work. In this case he'd hired a crew to replace the breakwall during the winter months when the canal authority opened the dam and lowered the lake in order to prevent spring flooding from rains and melting runoff, and he had instructed the crew leader to install a deadman every ten feet. Perhaps they had; he wouldn't know that for a fact until he stood in the water in daylight when he could inspect their exposed ends and count the number. But what he did see that should have been unavailable to his vision was the rectangular side of the nearest deadman. Each receding wave scoured it back to front, washing out gravel and dirt. The thick wooden tie was barely three feet in length; it should have been at least six, preferably eight. If his wife had accompanied him, he would have remarked, as he often had at the completion of a construction job performed by a contractor: *"I should have done the work myself. I could have screwed things up for a lot less money."* A self-deprecating sentiment, it was not intended to be taken on its face, as he rarely executed a task improperly.

He was not a man to seek counsel and instruction from others, Basteen—a fantasy writer who abided poor sales and rejection with stoicism because he believed evolution of any form or matter had little if anything to do with the constancy of time. He believed new phenomena could occur spontaneously if the elements of experience and exigency combined. He trusted unwaveringly that all metaphysics could change in an instant, the same as he had faith that a future book of his would be an overnight bestseller.

With the hour being what it was and the lake in an uproar, Basteen was surprised, once he turned his attention away from the deadman under assault, to see a small boat braving the waves. He bumped the car's headlights to high beam and the shrinking distance between the boat's own lights, forward and aft, suggested the craft was making an immediate though difficult turn in his direction. He silenced the engine, but left the headlights on, then worked his sinewy figure from out behind the steering wheel. As he stretched, he thought he heard a voice coming off the boat, but it was impossible to say for certain because of the water's own voice, which was loud and overrode other sounds.

The breeze this early summer night was stiff, persistent, unnaturally out of the east, and pleasantly warm. Likewise was the water this time of year increasingly warm and inviting, despite its currently obstreperous attitude. Even if his flesh hadn't felt sticky after the long, tortuous ride up from his home outside the city, Basteen would have stripped and immersed himself in the lake. He'd done it numerous times before.

Now standing naked at the edge where the breakwall ended and continuing to stretch his muscles, even emitting a primal scream to help unwind himself, he looked up at the night sky, hoping a bit more moonlight would push through the heavy layer of cloud so that he might better see the boat which, except for the small directional lights of white and green (momentarily red when it lost course), he could not make out at all. He judged it remained nearer the center of the lake than to himself and so, inhaling the moistened night air almost for the pure pleasure, he stepped off the shore. The next wave rolled in swiftly and crashed against his legs, hurling pebbles at the ankles and the barely encased fibulae. The rollover of water that was ushering oxygen to the lower depths had begun hours before his arrival. Proof was the pungent smell of vegetation and the corkscrew vallisneria mixed with the flying stone. He moved further out, treading gingerly to avoid slicing the underside of his feet on the razor-sharp, brittle shells of the tiny zebra mussels that covered every submerged rock like carpet nap, and each succeeding breaker knocked him back. Eventually, he advanced far enough and a swell lifted his one hundred-eighty pound body from the floor, whereupon it dove and slipped silently beneath the surface.

He ran like this, parallel to the shore, for about thirty meters, the water below him, a mere two fathoms; the turmoil above, less than half that. At the end of the run he reappeared, released the CO_2 from inside his lungs, breathed in new air effortlessly, and without hurry again submerged, sinking deeper to avoid the nudging of the swells. Much of a minute would pass until another gaseous exchange.

*

Several years earlier, a young local pilot fond of flying low and just off the lake's shoreline observed something moving through the water that he perceived to be a definite oddity. His first notion was he had seen a dolphin, and so he circled, not to confirm something he knew couldn't possibly be, but to clear his thinking and to show him what it must be: a freshwater sturgeon, a large bottom feeder often reported to exist in the deep lake, miraculously high above its comfort zone. But what he saw below the plane that afternoon was not a fish at all. A human being whose body in the water resembled a flexible torpedo was cutting through it, arcing and carving out its own wave band, fluid as the liquid itself. From that day forward, when he took to the sky, the pilot searched for this man as though Basteen were some kind of missing link.

Party guests at the writer's summer cottage were never so impressed by Basteen the Swimmer as the pilot of the Cessna was. Some who remained long into the night often entertained morbid expectations. They warned their host of snakes and of sudden

23

drop-offs that funneled a person to the coldest depths from which drowning victims were never recovered; a few of dangerous riptides, of which the lake was absent, the same as it was with sharks, a thing Basteen was indeed afraid of. They asked if he wasn't too drunk to play in water, reflecting their own condition more than his. They laughed when he trotted from the cottage naked, and they told him to watch out some hungry bass didn't mistake his endowment for a minnow or a popper, a useless remark as Basteen induced his penis to corrugate, a minor contribution to reduce drag. They considered him to be rather crazy than eccentric, and one night when the lake was calm and he was out a hundred meters, a visitor of this mind tried to take advantage. Ignorant of how sound traveled unencumbered across glassy water, the man said to Basteen's wife, "By the time we finish, it might not be infidelity."

*

Up he came, without splash, without a shake of the head. At the opposite shore the whitecaps sparkled. Overhead the cloudy sky opened as though splitting at a seam. The brilliant illumination spread by the moon soon captured the boat, and the swells on which the small craft rose and sank were in harmonic frequency with Basteen's own.

He recognized the boat, a wooden runabout, the only one of its size rigged with the mandated lighting for running at night, and he could see from its low profile that it had already taken on a great amount of water. But where was the boy, the boat's usual pilot? The girl alone seemed to be on board. She was on her knees at the stern, leaning as far forward from the transom as balance allowed. One hand worked the throttle arm of the motor while the other gripped the gunwale. The motor was sputtering and threatening to die.

As the seam further extended and broke above him, Basteen heard the girl shriek, then saw the boat's prow with its starboard green light point upward for a moment as though the craft were

24

about to shoot for the moon. But the weight of the outboard motor quickly drew it down and beneath the surface.

Basteen set out at once to rescue the girl, who was now struggling in the water, screaming for help. Yet no sign of rush marked his effort, as might be anticipated of a man on such a mission. In its place were pure economy and efficiency in both his stroke and powerful kick. And the undulation of his body as it sailed through wave after wave was all of a beautiful and perfect counterpoint. He no longer visualized himself as he once had while a teenager; no longer necessary was the out-of-body experience that had allowed him to coach himself and refine each movement. All motion in the water had been tamed, was always profoundly employed. Age alone was now the unknown influence. All the same, it was something he wanted noted, this early method of learning that had been so particular to himself, a method devoid of others' pedagogy and assistance; a method by which he stared and studied. Stared hard and long, and studied. He'd already abundant notes on himself in the event his publisher expressed interest in a personal memoir, an unlikely decision.

So, this for Basteen....

It had begun with an older brother who would enlist in, not the navy or the coast guard as the younger boy would have expected, but the army. In the many years since, Basteen never once altered his belief that, had he joined either of the other branches or gone to college and made the swim team, the brother's talent in water would have been discovered and he would have developed into not just an Olympian, but a great Olympian, an athlete to be honored and remembered long after his death. Basteen, just twelve, had watched whenever his sibling entered the community pool or the river. Then, later, prostrated in his bed or on the floor of his upstairs room, he attempted to imitate what he had observed. In time he was able to reshape his body, round the edges, shift more mass to the front, and turn his hands into a pair of broad cutting boards, just like the older boy's, although smaller.

One morning, he walked down to the river. It was a blustery

25

day of cold and rain, as he wanted; no one would be present to comment on his efforts, to offer critical advice as adults were often inclined. Neither would there be anyone on hand to save him from drowning if he failed in his trial run. But this second thought was hardly a consideration. A narrow tree-dappled island no more than a quarter-mile above the dam divided the river, and Basteen had once watched his brother leave the shore, fight the current, and reach the island in just twelve strokes. That day in September, with no other soul around, Basteen arrived there in twenty.

Soon after, his brother was bused to boot camp, then shipped overseas. Basteen, again under his own tutelage, began to study fish, sea mammals, and amphibians. He chose the dolphin for his model. He had already learned to round himself in front; he next added a dorsal curvature. And while his entire body would never breach like a whale, his feet in the water would begin to function like flukes.

*

The girl was fighting to stay afloat; and at the crest of every parabola in Basteen's rolling continuum through the four-foot waves, the eye, in the air for only a second, locked onto her position. Another thirty meters and he would have her in his grasp and move them both to land.

Except she weakened. She disappeared from view.

With scarcely a pause Basteen took in a fresh breath and angled deep. The lake, strikingly clear water even before the invasion of the filtering mussels, permitted greater penetration of the moonlight as the turbidity was stretching only slowly from the shore, and Basteen could see the girl, mostly by a white kerchief knotted about her neck. She appeared lifeless. And she was beginning to tumble, a signal that both were near the end of the underwater shelf, which, according to the navigation chart on the wall of his cottage, would give way precipitously to a depth well beyond a hundred meters.

Too much time would elapse before he could get her to the

shore; the realization came to him suddenly that she could not be revived. Not in the water. She was irretrievably lost to this life. Yet the recovery of her young body was an obligation he could not overlook. Otherwise, she would drift to the very lowest depths where the water's perpetually cold temperatures denied a corpse the ugly bloating that could raise it back to the surface and release it to the loved ones left behind.

*

And now is when Basteen hesitates. He weighs that animal class which, long ago, was decreed upon him. Although he has taught himself to reduce his heart rate, thereby allowing an extended stay underwater, still, he can but estimate the time it will take to raise the girl's body. And what if his estimation is wrong? Or what if his flesh becomes snagged on a piece of debris that sits for all eternity at the dark bottom?

Then he, too, will drown.

Faithful to his idiosyncrasy, Basteen resumes the descent and calls upon his mind, a dusty section of it holding specialized knowledge. He opens his mouth and lets the water rush in to flood the cavity. Then clamping the lips tight against each other, he draws inward on his cheeks so as to put the water under great pressure. He can only imagine where the opercula are hidden, and he pictures them, rightly or wrongly, just behind the ears.

For now his air continues to remain good and he is swimming well, but his mammal's lungs are certain to burn if one gas cannot be traded for another. It is a million years of ossified cartilage under the skin that he is striving to crack. If he succeeds, the rest will follow—the filaments and lamellae—he feels certain of that, and the exchange, made. And so, aware there is no turning back, he brings greater pressure to bear on the oxygen-rich water trapped in his mouth.

The shelf has fallen away completely and the kerchief is ever graying in the diminishing moonlight. It is all that is available to Basteen's eyes. Soon enough it will surrender all color and turn to black. In the meantime, he dives ever deeper, expecting a tremor.

CRUSHER RUN

It's a cold night to be riding a motorcycle on the interstate, and Ezra has three hundred miles ahead of him. The temperature will dip further because the bike is pointed north. The Impala would have been his choice, with its heater, but it sits in the shop because of a computer malfunction that was causing the loss of power—yet another item of modern life that, like the marriages of his son and daughter, favors whole replacement of the module as the method of repair. And while either of his neighbors and any of his friends would have been only too glad to lend him a car, he has never been a borrower of money, tools, implements, or anything. As for the old pickup, it is sunk on its rear axle because a ton of crusher run lies in the bed, hundreds of pounds above Detroit's rating for the vehicle. Shoveling the stone off into the potholes of his long dirt lane just wasn't an option; he'd worked all day like a penned-up wild dog. He was too tired.

Which was a concern when he'd left, one hour after learning the news. All the time it took to clean up a little, call the kids on the coast, and collect his leather jacket and gloves, favorite riding boots, helmet, a change of clothes, whiskey flask. Still, there wasn't an alternative. She could die at any moment. The trooper hadn't said that, he didn't have to. Under the circumstances both knew he didn't have to. Between the worry and the cold he believes he'll stay awake. Anyway, who's ever heard of a biker falling asleep.

He'd bought the motorcycle with her encouragement, a new touring model for which he paid cash. The year was 1995.

"You've always wanted to see the country," she said, "and I know you've wanted to do it on a motorcycle. Now's the time. Anna and Little Ezra are on their own, and you've still got your health."

"Well sure, Else," he said hesitantly, "but what about you? You'd like to see the country, wouldn't you? I figured maybe we could swing ourselves a small motor home, or even a van and have it customized."

Oh, the grin that day, so big and unrevealing. He's never forgotten it. And then she disappeared from the stove where she was frying eggs, and before he could finish "Where are you going?" she was back, still grinning, only now from the inside of a brilliantly white, visorless helmet. He couldn't help but drop his head and laugh. Not loud, just laugh. She was something else, she'd always been.

And she wasn't done. She next pushed him onto one of the stools at the breakfast nook and slid another behind him for herself. She wrapped her arms around his waist, which despite middle age remained more muscle than belly.

"That time Ezra, Jr. considered getting one to save on gas, you told him they were too dangerous," he reminded her.

"I know, and that hasn't changed," she said. "But if we were to crash and die, it's not like he or Anna would be losing their children."

As cold as it is tonight on the four-lane highway now leading him through higher elevations where bowls of fog are forming in the valleys, this memory produces a tear that is distinguishable from the rest of the water in his eyes brought on by his rushing through the chilly air.

But her enthusiasm that day hadn't entirely convinced him she would enjoy traveling around the country on two wheels.

"You know we won't be staying in a motel every night," he warned as she returned to the eggs. "Most nights we'll camp. Pitch a tent if the weather calls for it. Otherwise, we'll be bedding down in sleeping bags right out in the open. Not at a campground either, except when we get too ripe for each other and need to shower."

She smiled, turned back toward him. "Do you know there are sections on the Snake River, Ezra, where, if you jump in, you'll be ten feet downstream before you can count one thousand and one?"

Snake River...?

He really wished he had the words to tell her how much he loved her. So many things about her. There was never anything not

30

to love.

*

The first outings were day trips. "We both need to season our butts," he had said, and off they went to circle a few of the small lakes that were on the map but which they'd never seen, to visit a museum in the city and a couple of wineries on the way, to travel to an air show and a popular mushroom festival.

She had never been a querulous partner, but following those early trips, she got across to him that staring into his back wasn't the best for taking in the scenery. He was broad-shouldered and taller than her by several inches. He quickly fixed the problem by replacing the long double seat with a single saddle for himself and a built-up, cushioned pillion for her. When next she climbed aboard, she not only could see what he was seeing in the road ahead and the distance beyond, but she also was able to talk into his ear without always shouting.

*

Without a watch, Ezra surmises the time is well after midnight because the cars are mostly gone and the behemoth transports have taken over the road. Up until a few minutes ago, the motorcycle was cruising at seventy, but a mile back he saw a deer near the shoulder and more are certain to appear. Plus the fog, thickening and beginning to spread like lava, swallowed the guiding taillights of an eighteen-wheeler. At the moment he is feathering the throttle, trying to keep his speed at forty, but more often letting it drop to under thirty. It's just impossible to see.

He wants to keep thinking of her, because if there are forces at work in matters of life and death, forces that can alter starts and finishes, he wants the God behind them to know how deeply in love they are and always have been, to realize a mistake might be in the making that is not in the best interest of life on this earth. But facing unsafe conditions, he must concentrate, think hard about what he is doing; otherwise, like her, he could end up in the

31

I.C. unit of a hospital.

He throttles down further because he's starting to jerk the handlebar, fooled that the road is angled one direction when it's the opposite. The dense moisture in the air is collecting on his face, dribbling down his neck and inside the leather jacket and layered shirts. He can feel his feet growing wet as well. It makes him colder, and he shivers.

The muster of fog onto the darkened landscape finally thins in waves, and just like that, he is out of it, and his vision is magically extended. Ahead is a rural exit. He pulls off.

After filling the tank on the bike, he goes inside the Marathon and picks out a couple of candy bars for later. The attendant looks him over as he tugs out his wallet. "Coffee's free with the fill-up." Ezra shakes his head, replies, "No time."

Outside again, beside the pump, he opens one of the fiberglass saddlebags and finds the flask. He stands next to the front tire and windshield, staring up at the interstate, taking a few swigs. The whiskey courses through a body like coffee doesn't, and he shivers once more, only this is the welcome kind. He returns the flask to the bag, swaddling it with his underwear, and then it's back aboard the bike.

*

The first of the longer trips in both time-on-the-road and mileage took them to the coastal beaches of the Florida panhandle—a week with the overly warm Gulf water, six days for down and back. Then, before that summer was officially over, they returned to the beach, only this time in South Carolina where they also spent a day with their daughter, who seemed unsure what to make of her aging parents riding a motorcycle. The next year, there was no actual destination. Instead, they avoided the interstates and traveled through the river towns along the Mississippi, and in several summers to follow they took similar journeys, including ones along the Grand Army of the Republic Highway and old Route 40 with its cracked macadam. Mostly they toured and camped alone, but on occasion they met other bikers and traveled with them for hundreds of miles, as they'd done with Jasper and Lucy who were their age and with whom they became friends. Then two years ago, he announced to her his biggest surprise, and didn't she announce her own right back.

"Want to know where I think we should go this summer? Come July, when it's as close to a guarantee as you can get there won't be snow, I think we should head west to the Rockies and the Snake River." And for a joke, he pointed his eyes at the floor, then moved them rapidly to the right, as though she had just leaped into the river and was being swept away by the current.

"Ezra," she said. "I don't want to ride with you anymore."

*

The candy bars are gone, the flask empty, he's wet and freezing and wondering why hypothermia hasn't set in. His hands feel like cold steel. For a while he was flexing them, but when that failed to boost the circulation, he began reaching down and cupping them around the transverse cylinder heads, holding on for a minute or more, first one, then the other, absorbing heat from the engine. But this, too, no longer works.

The sky remains dark, but morning is approaching. There's an increase in vehicles, and the big trucks are rushing so they can be off-loaded first, or at least without the normal delays, by the morning shifts. Glancing at the odometer, he estimates another hour of riding.

Her expression, he remembers, fooled him. He'd read fear in her face and thought maybe their close call on the previous trip was the reason. They'd topped a rise at a speed too fast for the unexpected sharp bend on the other side, and he instinctively leaned as much as his mind would allow, while pushing hard on one grip and pulling up on the other. And just as they were coming out of the curve with not an inch of pavement to spare, another surprise. Six, seven, maybe more—he never did go back to count how many—tractor tires were rolling off the end of a flatbed truck

33

and bouncing directly at them like bandits on a tear. There was nothing to do but brace and take the hits. And hit they did, three of them, thick knobby donuts of black rubber that rocked and jolted them all over. The bike wanted to go down, but with all his farm work strength he managed to keep it upright. When the ordeal was over, they were staring into a deep open embankment.

"Why not?" he asked her. "Else, is something wrong?"

"Ezra, I want to ride alongside, behind, or ahead of you. I don't want to sit on the back anymore."

It took him more than a moment to realize she was asking for a motorcycle of her own to operate. Then, surprising her further, and maybe himself too, he replied, "You're on the short side. We'll have to look around to find one with a seat set low enough so your feet can touch the ground."

And that was pretty much that! Two months later, they were touring the Rocky Mountains on separate machines and scaring the daylights out of themselves with a dip in one of the swiftest stretches of the Snake River.

*

Throughout the long night the air has been motionless, stirred only by the hurtling vehicles. Now it is beginning to stir of its own. Short gusts coming out of the west sporadically strike Ezra and attempt to shove the motorcycle and him off the roadway. He prays rain isn't in the offing.

Of course it's much too late to wish she hadn't gone, but he can't stop himself from wondering. Perhaps he should have been less agreeable. What if he would have said, "I wish you wouldn't, Else"? Might she have decided to stay home? It was four hundred miles to Lucy's, not a trivial jaunt for someone motorcycling alone her first time. Still, it was a sonovabitch who ran a red light. And that happened every day all across the country at thousands of intersections.

Afraid of a weather change for the worse, he now cracks the throttle. The bike rapidly eats up the concrete between itself and a pair of taillights; a red, white, and blue garbage truck, and the motorcycle's by in an instant. He doesn't let off, racing around a dawdling empty church bus and a compact car with a bent frame, then a dump truck and a van, and another dump truck. Next up, a tractor-trailer. Only it is barreling, and considerable time passes before the motorcycle creeps alongside the double rear wheels. The diesel's powerful roar from the belly is the first embrace to reach Ezra, joined by a moving cone of unexpected heat. He gives in freely to the surprise as it warms the body's insides, dries its flesh, thins the blood that's turned to syrup, invigorates his every cell like the first beautiful day after a long winter. He rides in this wonderful pocket for he doesn't know how long, and he can see the driver of the truck looking in his mirror again and again, and he knows what the man is thinking, but it doesn't matter, not to Ezra whose biggest concern is to safely reach his injured wife; and a body that isn't frozen, isn't tensed, will help insure he does. He'll linger in the warmth for as long as possible.

Yet, no sooner is the thought completed, a violent blast of air from the left jerks the motorcycle to within inches of the truck, and an all-out ripping crosswind arises. The warmth comforting Ezra is gone in an instant, torn away, shifted to the other side.

For a time he maintains his speed, hoping the heat will return. But it does not. The wind persists like the dedicated courier of change it often is, and what Ezra now feels he soon will know.

RIPARIAN RITE

This summer at the lake, Thurman wishes he were like the dogs. Three of them, and not a one raises its head from slumber and barks an objection to any noise on the water, except if a bass boat ventures close and bumps against an outer piling of the empty slip. Then the sound is a kind not often heard, a hollow rumbling, and the trio breaks into its racket, whereupon he looks up from his book and adds his own noise by shouting at them to shut up.

In the past he and Julia have been able to get away to the lake house for eight weeks, but this year they were resigned to thinking in terms of days, and sixteen are all they have, which explains why the intrusions are annoying. Eight weeks or sixteen days, the work required to ready the property for seasonal living is the same: clear the pump of the foul-tasting pink antifreeze and the suction line of stale lake water; vacuum up the annual supply of dead ants; take a broom to the windows and knock out the wasp nests and numerous spider webs; rake down the prodigious volume of slimy leaves from the steps leading to the upper parking spots; scrub the mildew from the dock, then nail down the wind-torn corrugated sheets forming the roof of the boat slip; and this time-around Thurman will have to muck out the basement because flooding, resulting from spring rains, has left behind a mess, including a dead mud puppy.

But none of this does he mind, nor does Julia; and although she insists, with the exception of clearing the water lines, they do the tasks throughout their stay rather than rush to accomplish them all in the first few days as is the normal strategy, the maintenance is expected. The same as are the dive-bombing swallows that attack them for an entire morning and afternoon before concluding that the two dock lizards on the beach towels will not slither up to the flying couple's nest inside the slip and snatch away their fledglings.

Julia, who is straightening the ends of her towel with one hand and tweaking the nose of their smallest dog, a mutt, with the other, asks, "Honey, are you wishing now you brought the boat?"

"What you mean is," Thurman says, "you're wishing we did."

"Well, I like the boat, certainly. But don't you? Don't you enjoy tooling up and down the shore?" She is trim, too pale for the warm months of summer; and her hand makes the movement of a slithering snake when she says "tooling."

He looks at her and knows he does. But then again, he doesn't. He hasn't towed along the 18-footer open-bow with the 175-horse I/O this summer because he didn't think the 600 miles up and back would be worth the effort for the short stay. But in a moment of truthfulness, he knows also that he has no need for any boat, period, and the reason for this is buried in his past: he grew up among people with boats whose motors were forever on the fritz. His brother's best friend who had operated a popular gas station and owned four, which were in various states of disrepair, once said, "Thurmie, if you ever want to get even with someone, don't think about beating them up. Don't think about burning a bag of dog turds on their porch. Just give them a boat."

Their boat, despite a used purchase, is fairly new, and when he is again truthful, Thurman admits it runs problem-free. This actually may be a contributing factor to the noise, he thinks: today's watercraft are greatly improved descendants of the troublesome things he knew as a child. Not only are more recreational powerboats than ever racing across waterways all over, but also they just aren't breaking down with the frequency he remembers, thus permitting them to stay out longer. And if you were to make a present of one to an enemy in this day and age, it will never occur to that person you are seeking revenge.

For Julia, the noise coming off the lake is not the irritation it is to her husband. As the editor-in-chief for a university press, she welcomes the break for her tired eyes and passes time either tanning on the dock or swimming laps back and forth along the shoreline. If she reads anything, it is usually a popular magazine for women. But it is different with Thurman who also loves to read but can find little opportunity to do so during the rest of the year.

In previous summers prior to their departure, he visited their local bookseller and purchased a dozen or so titles gone to paperback. This time he has brought along half that number.

Day Three of the vacation is when he grows sufficiently annoyed to act. It is Thurman's perfect setting for enjoying the lake and reading a book. The morning is bright, the water calm, the air quiet. An occasional bass breaks the water to snatch a passing fly. The swallows acrobatically capture hundreds of others. Inside, Julia is gobbling up ants with the bagless, but the job takes just twenty minutes and the vacuum cleaner is soon silent. On rising that morning Thurman informed her his intention was to sit on the dock and read for a few hours, then hose the mud out of the basement because, like the ants, "it isn't a task you want to put off for too long." But before he is three pages into Larry McMurtry's *Comanche Moon,* the familiar blue-striped cigarette boat from last year is disturbing the pleasant atmosphere. With its exhaust pipe above the water, the stentorian throatiness of the engine is an abomination to the natural serenity. The long slender craft roars past Thurman not a quarter mile from where he lounges, blasting his psyche and his ears, and he continues to hear the motor when it is out of sight around a southerly point. He watches and eventually contents himself with believing the sound will soon diminish to nothing as the craft continues its course, and the tranquility of the lake will return. Only the thought is premature as the boat suddenly swings around and he can hear it start back in his direction. For the next hour the deafening boat stays within range of Thurman who, angry that anyone would choose to pollute the lake's peaceful character, slams down his book and leaves the dock for the dirty basement.

The mud accumulation on the floor has remained moist because the house was closed throughout the spring, and Thurman hoses it clean without scrubbing. The cigarette boat is soon out of hearing to the north from whence it originally arrived, and Thurman, eager to return to his novel now that all is quiet again, grabs the squeegee and forces the remaining water into the floor drain. But the boat, like a dogged horsefly, reappears.

Now, as it approaches, a furious Thurman dashes to the basement doorway, where he stops and carefully lays a bead. It is hard to judge the distance over the mirror-like surface—300 yards, maybe?—and the extended arm first elevates a foot above the boat, then swings ahead of the bow as he realizes he will need to lead because of the speed.

Appearing from the side of the house, Julia steps in front of the doorway and blocks his line of fire.

"What did you do with the mud puppy?" she inquires with arms akimbo, while looking approvingly at the drying floor.

Without allowing his focus to stray from the fast-moving target, Thurman uses a finger from the hand out front to point at some upturned earth near the side of the house.

Julia then turns away to face the lake. The boat is now beyond their frontage and out of Thurman's range, when it shifts to warp speed and triples in decibels. She turns back, grinning, and reaches out to push the squeegee's handle toward the ground.

"Guess who just arrived for summer fun," she says. "The Kirchgrabers."

The immediate *Oh no!* is on his face, and she laughs.

"What are they doing here? They should have already come and gone by this date."

"In the past there have been two Kirchgraber families...? This year, Honey, there are three. Twelve kids altogether."

Now she can see the *Oh no!* has been replaced by an obscenity that he would like to voice, but she knows he will not.

"And besides the boat, Thurman, this year they've brought along a jet ski."

"Why do you think this is funny?" he asks. "If you had to read manuscripts at work under these conditions, you wouldn't think it's so funny."

"But I don't. And so it is." She tweaks his cheek.

The Kirchgrabers are quick to chop up both the water and the air. The next day, beginning at sun-up, the boat is pulling skiers and tubers and kids kneeling on tiny boards, first singularly, then in pairs, finally in threes. The lake is forty miles long and two-and-a-half miles wide, but the Kirchgrabers spend all day on the water within narrow range of Thurman. Try as he does to ignore the boat motor and the screaming children, by two o'clock he has lost all concentration and sets aside his story, this one written by an old classmate, a novel whose title *An Absence of Spine,* he thinks, might be speaking to him.

This time it is the steps leading to the parking spaces high above that he attacks. He rakes the huge collection of last autumn's leaves from the top toward the bottom. When he pauses at a middle landing, the boat rushes by his dock, and behind it, cutting across its wake, is the jet ski.

Thurman stares at the small raucous machine while it streaks to the middle of the lake. There it makes a wide sweep and again slices across the boat's wake. It is racing for all it's worth right at Thurman's dock. *Too easy,* he thinks, as the target is driving straight at him and he is looking down upon it. Quickly, he lays a bead. But just when he is about to release, the Kirchgraber aboard the machine throws a hand overhead and waves. Instinctively, Thurman lowers the rake and waves back, even as he is disappointed by his innate friendliness. And then, to double the disappointment, the Kirchgraber, he realizes, is waving not at him, but at Julia on the dock, and she is returning the gesture. As the jet ski buzzes off, she turns, smiling, and throws Thurman a kiss.

Each evening Thurman attempts to read his books, but always he remains annoyed from the day's intrusions so that concentration is still a problem. Finally, two days before the vacation is to end, an idea strikes him. The oldest Kirchgraber has informed him there are no fishing tournaments scheduled, so that he can expect fewer morning anglers, maybe none. He reminds himself that first light is around 5, and at 4:30 he rises. All three dogs rise, too, and follow him into the outer room where they resume their sleep. Ah, it is wonderfully quiet, and Thurman puts on his glasses, opens the book.

Chapters one, two, three, four. Before long, chapter eight. Seventy-two pages, and the entire book only 270. Feeling good, he jumps into the next chapter, mostly dialogue. Before long he is re-reading lines. What is in his head is not what's on the page.

Looking up, he sees a slim bass boat has drifted near the slip and one of its fishermen is cursing because he has hooked his jig in a piling. It is too much for Thurman, and once again he lays a bead.

"No way we can replace the screen in that window before leaving," says Julia. She has stepped into the outer room. Groggy from sleep but ever intellectually alert, she drags herself over to Thurman and takes the eyeglasses from his hand. "Trading in the rifles for a handgun, I see."

He bubbles silent laughter, but asks seriously, "Do I worry you?"

"You?" Julia rubs her eyes and widens them. "Not at all." Pointing the glasses at the bass boat beyond the screen, she pulls the trigger. When nothing happens, she appears to frown, and Thurman watches as she turns them over in her hand. Just for a moment, he wonders if it's the safety she is searching for.

UNVISITED SPACES

Watching one of the morning news shows, Ritchie Lee Whelan burst out laughing.

"Alison, you got to hear this!"

Alison Keene appeared from the bedroom, in a hurry.

"I'm running late for work, and there's a deposition first thing. I have to go."

"That Dr. Emily? She said if we find a tick on Churchill, we should take it to Dr. Bernice. You know, to check for that fruity disease?"

"Oh, those crazy New Yorkers," said Alison. "But that disease hasn't a thing to do with fruit, Ritchie."

"Don't I know that. It's not even spelled the same."

Last evening, while sitting on the front porch, the pair had picked off more than thirty ticks buried in the long coat of Ritchie Lee's red-haired mutt and deposited them in a jar half-filled with bleach. Some were already dead from the poison squeezed days before into the nape of the dog's neck, but there were others still alive who, in Ritchie's words, were "mapping out the territory of ol' Churchill's hide." Ritchie Lee wished he could run up the Bluegrass Parkway to the airport and hop a flight to some New York City medical clinic where he would drop the jar of the now whitened bloodsuckers onto the doctor's desk with a note that read, "Compliments of Dr. Emily and CBS."

"What are your plans for today?" asked Alison as she hunted the car key inside her purse. "Do you have any water deliveries scheduled? Or anything?"

"With last week's rain, just one. Jarboe's Mexican Hotel," said Ritchie Lee. "Then, when I get back, I thought I might start on those bookshelves you want."

"Oh, Ritchie, no. Don't do that. I've been thinking of something a little different from what I told you. I'm thinking bookshelves, yes, but now with maybe a cabinet or two underneath for the DVD and the rest."

"So?"

"You'll need a router more than ever."

"I could buy one."

"And you're planning to do this with those saws in your pickup?"

"I'll look around for a used table or miter saw. Dudes buy them all the time, thinking they'll build houses and do remodeling. Afterwards, the things sit around and rust."

"I really have to go," said Alison. "Yesterday they shut down a lane on the parkway and lowered the speed limit to forty-five to protect the workers. There were police watching, too." She pecked his lips with a perfunctory kiss.

Ritchie Lee went back to the television after she was gone, but Dr. Emily was off the air. Alison's own doctor would laugh when he told her the story about the ticks. Those folks living in New York couldn't resist their digs at the South. Mostly it showed up in commercials: *"Pleeze pass the jelly!"* But once in a while they made a mistake and showed themselves to be the bozo.

He stepped over to where she wanted the bookshelves and, taking his tape measure off the television, measured the dimensions for the tenth time, but he still didn't jot down the numbers. What's wrong with the bookshelves they had found at an absolute auction, he thought, and why not drive out to another Saturday auction and bid on a few more? No, she was insisting on shelves built right against the walls, floor to ceiling, with special platforms at the corner, where they would intersect, to display her grandmother's figurines. *And now she wants cabinets!* Ritchie Lee thought about this for a long time, unsure if wanting a cabinet and shelves was really what it was about. Or was she trying to make the project so complicated that he would give it up? He once told her that he would do anything for her. He had told this to a couple of other women, too, and he had meant it. With Alison, he wasn't so sure. Too often he felt she saw him as her parents did. Not that either ever said anything to his face, but it was written all over theirs. It was their daughter's house, she was paying the mortgage

44

and the taxes, and they didn't like his living there scot-free, even though it was Alison's idea that he move in. (*"Let's see if I can stand you all day everyday before discussing marriage,"* she'd said with a half-hearted laugh.) Anyway, it wasn't true, he wasn't a sponge, and that's what pissed him off. He worked when work was available, and he had already filled out applications at a dozen places, including GE in Louisville and Toyota in Georgetown; and the money he brought in, he spent freely on Alison and their needs. Hadn't he returned from Kroger's earlier this week with two hundred dollars worth of groceries? When he finished the water hauling this morning, he would hop in the pickup and head over to the Danville Lowe's and buy them a router and some bits. She probably thought having to use a router would prevent him from doing the project; this morning was the third time she'd mentioned the tool. She didn't want shelving with cleats for support, she'd said; she wanted the shelves to slide into the uprights. "What you want is a *dado*," he told her. He'd done a little reading on the subject, and that word *dado* had taken hold.

*

The truck for water hauling was an old Jimmy painted red, no shine. The cylindrical tank was black with matching no-shine, and was severely rusting on one end along the weld. A pair of thick chains and binders secured it to the truck frame. The tank's capacity was 2,400 gallons and the weight of the load tested the truck's engine and brakes, not to mention the driver's mettle, on every hill and holler. Ritchie Lee had purchased it off old Dick Robb, whose son told his father he wasn't interested in driving across people's lawns and filling their cisterns. But Ritchie Lee now thought he might have been bested, which was the reason he was searching for work elsewhere. The day following the exchange of Robb's title to the truck and Ritchie Lee's personal check, the weekly *Sun* appeared with the headline, "WATERLINE TO EXTEND TO ENTIRE COUNTY BEFORE YEAR'S END." And no time was being wasted. Along several roads he was already seeing the evidence, mile-long mounds of upturned clay and rock ribboning up and down the rolling terrain, as if some cartoony woodchuck, rather than a backhoe, were behind the digging, which meant it would all be finished in a mere few minutes, not several months, and folks would convert their cisterns into patios, while others, like Jarboe maybe, would turn their farmland into a trailer park.

He downshifted and rolled the truck to the rear of the Corner Store where the large overhead hose was hanging. He hoped the automatic mechanism was fixed; he didn't want to drive another twelve miles into Springfield for water. There was no money to be made if you were forced to do that.

He jumped down out of the truck and went inside to ask for quarters. That the young girl behind the counter accepted his two dollars told him the dispensing mechanism was repaired and he wouldn't have to go elsewhere.

From a booth in the rear Len Robb saw him, and the tall farm boy rose up out of it, a styrofoam coffee in hand. Ritchie Lee expected him to ask how things were going with the truck and the water hauling. Instead, Robb asked, "Have you heard about Carly?"

There was only one woman from the area named Carly, and Ritchie Lee had loved her very much.

"Carly? No. What about her?"

"She's missing."

"What do you mean?"

"It was on the news this morning. She went out jogging yesterday evening and never came back."

Jogging. That was a big part of the reason she had stopped seeing him. She would run almost every day for an hour or two, and she wanted him to run with her. But it wasn't in him. Running, jogging, or whatever people called it, it wasn't something he could make himself do.

"She never came back?"

"Do you know her husband?"

Ritchie Lee nodded. "Just to see him. Seems like a nice fellow."

"Well, according to him, she always ran up 53 a ways and then turned onto Biddle Ridge where there's no traffic and it's safer."

"Huh..."

"Yeah, right," said Robb, frowning.

"That's all that's known?"

"That's all I've heard."

The girl behind the counter said, "There's more. It was just on the radio. They found tire tracks and some signs of where there may have been a struggle. Police think she might have been abducted."

Ritchie Lee watched Robb shake his head at the floor.

Outside, behind the store, he slipped the quarters into the slot and commenced to flood the black tank with chlorinated city water. As the level rose inside, the hollow sound of deep, dark metal lessened. Once the tank was full, he climbed back behind the wheel and headed up 53 toward the Jarboe farm and the Mexicans. When he reached Carly's house, he looked over, but it appeared silent, despite several SUVs and pickups filling the driveway. He moved his eyes from the road to the sloping sides beyond her property. But what was he hoping to find, he asked himself. He could think only the worst. Beautiful women never came out of these things alive. He wondered if at that very moment she was already dead. And why hadn't her husband been jogging with her? Didn't she tell him that a prerequisite a man intending to marry her must fulfill is that he exercise too?

At Biddle Ridge, he gazed down its narrow pavement, but made no move to turn off. She wouldn't be discovered along 53 and no one would find her on the side of Biddle Ridge either. If she were found at all, it would be somewhere else, where no one would expect. He drove on toward his delivery point, all the while thinking of her. She was a year and two months older than him. He remembered how soft her skin was. All this time—what, three

47

years already?—and he could still feel her flesh as if the recollection wasn't one at all, but was real. It was one of the many things about her he had found fascinating. So much hard exercise, and yet so soft.

Going uphill, the truck strained, and the engine and transmission noise inside the cab was deafening. He turned onto a gravel road a mile before snaky route 53 met the parkway and followed it to the Jarboe farm. It was a warm spring morning, sunny, and a few redbuds still had a flower or two. He swung a wide turn alongside the trailer, then backed up to the cistern. Several Mexican men were outside and another opened the door upon his arrival. Inside he could see a woman and a young child. It was impossible to know how many lived in the trailer, which his buddies had nicknamed the Mexican Hotel, but it was understandable how Jarboe scheduled him to come out with a load every three or four days, more during dry spells.

None of the men spoke much English and he couldn't speak but a couple words of Spanish. When he listened to them talk among themselves, their language seemed like it was traveling at light speed. He wondered if they had their own brand of *you know,* or *ah,* or *well.* As a few moseyed over to watch him unload the water into the cistern, he thought of the joke he'd told Alison, how one day, when the world announced that people from all over the globe now spoke English, America would respond with "Sorry, we switched to Spanish." He thought that idea funny, but Alison wouldn't crack a smile.

He couldn't blame them for coming here. None of the politicians on their side of the border seemed to be doing much to make life better for them in their own country, and too many here didn't want to do the hard work anymore, like kill chickens and cut tobacco.

One of the younger men came closer and bent over to look into the bottom of the cistern as it was filling and the motley debris and decaying bugs were roiling the water. He carried a long ugly scar under his chin, and Ritchie Lee again thought of Carly and

what might have happened to her. He knew what Alison would say
to what he was thinking, but the fellow in Lexington who killed the
boyfriend of a university co-ed a year ago was a migrant, and
Jarboe certainly had not traveled down to the border to interview
these people. He looked at each of the faces, and those that were
friendly may have keyed into his thoughts, for their smiles
disappeared. He ignored them after this, drained and recoiled the
dispensing hose, replaced the cap on the concrete cistern, then
drove off, the old truck grinding its way back toward 53.

*

As he returned to the house, Churchill raced out from behind
the purple lilac that needed pruning and attacked the truck's tires.
They stepped together toward the front door of the house where the
dog wanted to follow him inside.

Ritchie Lee said, "Not this time of year." Leaning over, he
walked his fingers through the animal's coat, parting the hair at the
follicles. A new army of the tiny bloodsuckers had assembled in
and around the dog's ears and eyes, with others heading for the
same destination. "How come they always party on your head,
Churchill? How come they never show up on your ass?"

Inside, he saw by the DVD's digital clock that it was noon,
which surprised him, and he clicked on the television to a
Lexington station. This thing about Carly wasn't really setting in,
and the story, as reported, offered nothing new to push him in any
direction. He wished he could do something, but what? Others
were already searching for her, the reason so many vehicles were
present at her house, and the same reason he hadn't seen any faces.
But it would be fruitless, he again told himself, and they all would
soon give up—if they hadn't already—after learning of the tire
tracks and the signs that Carly had fought with her attacker. He
turned off the television and stared at the space where the
bookshelves were to go.

Carly, in spite of drifting from her church, had remained
spiritual the same as he, but it was otherwise with her family and

49

friends; and Ritchie Lee was sure some of them were busy forming a prayer chain while he stood around thinking about an electric tool. It didn't seem right to go out on this day and purchase a router. But neither did he want to be available to receive their call. He wanted nothing to do with a prayer chain and holding hands with people he might not like. If he prayed, it would be silently and alone.

And realizing that praying was something he could do, he raised his head and offered up a brief one, but with little belief it would work. So then he offered another that he thought might possibly be successful, although it was really a kind of postscript to the first. Afterwards, he left the house to run the pickup over to Lowe's in the next county, throwing Churchill in the cab for company. But to avoid answering the phone he might better have stayed at the house and worked outside. At the huge home improvement store, the routers, each with its own special features, price, and rebate, were too much for him as he thought about an old girlfriend, and he was unable to reach a decision. To make the matter worse, another customer approached and informed him, almost in secret, that one of the store's competitors in Lexington would match the price, plus return the purchaser another ten percent. "You'd be foolish to buy it here," the man whispered to Ritchie Lee.

On the return trip he pulled the pickup into a McDonald's and shared a quarter-pounder with the dog. It was late afternoon when he was once again at Alison's, who returned from work not long after.

"You've heard about Carly?" she said after coming through the door.

He just nodded.

Aware that Ritchie Lee once dated the missing woman before her marriage to another man, Alison didn't know what else to say, so she disappeared into the bedroom to change into other clothes.

"I didn't buy the router," she listened to him report. "Churchill and I drove over to Danville and I looked at them, but I couldn't make up my mind."

She didn't offer an immediate response. Instead, she finished ridding herself of her work outfit and slid into jeans and a yellow boatneck.

When she again joined him in the front room, she said, "I'm glad you didn't buy the router. I have someone coming out in just a few minutes."

"Coming out? To do what? You've hired someone to build your bookshelves, haven't you? You don't think I can. That's what it is, isn't it?"

"Ritchie, I know you can build them. But it will take you much longer than it will Miguel."

"Miguel?"

"Miguel Lugo."

"You've hired a migrant? Well, I imagine cutting tobacco is a lot like cutting a dado," he said with deliberate sarcasm.

"Miguel is an American. He's lived in Kentucky nearly all his life and he speaks better English than most of us. What's more, Ritchie, he's a cabinetmaker. That's what he does for a living."

"Where did you find him?"

"He's a client. He's been working for someone else for years. Our office is doing the paperwork so he can incorporate and become his own employer."

They heard the vehicle on the gravel driveway and Alison went to the door to wait. A middle-aged man, who would have struck anyone immediately as a hard worker, stepped out of his truck and strode up the sidewalk while glancing at the property.

"This is a beautiful place you have," Miguel Lugo said to Alison when he was inside the house. She quickly made the introductions and Ritchie Lee extended a hand.

"It's a pleasure to meet you," said Lugo. "Now, where are these shelves to go, as I'm sure you both would like to relax after working all day?"

The question was addressed to Alison, but it was Ritchie Lee who answered.

"Right over there," he said. "They'll stretch from the window to the corner, and from there along the wall to the other window."

"But in the corner I want a few shelves to display some things other than books," explained Alison. "Things like crystal. And I want glass doors over them for protection while allowing them still to be viewed."

"You had mentioned cabinets this morning," said Lugo.

"Underneath," said Alison. "For the components. Maybe include the TV too."

Lugo ignored them as he studied the walls and the windows without taking a measurement. After a time, he moved his gaze to the other walls and also to locations nearer the center of the room.

"What's the matter?" inquired Ritchie Lee. "Are you thinking the shelves should be built elsewhere? Maybe leave that space where Alison wants them for something else?"

Lugo shook his head. "Along any wall is fine," he said. "It's all unvisited space. What I am looking for is a spot on the opposite side of the room for a smaller cabinet that will balance and pull everything together."

"Oh," said Alison, liking the idea of a second cabinet off by itself.

"*'Unvisited space,'* what's that mean?" Ritchie Lee asked, curious.

Lugo produced a measuring tape and returned to the location for the shelves.

"Come over here," he ordered them both. "Now look where you stopped," he said, pointing to their feet with the extended yellow tape. "You're each about a foot from the wall."

"So what?" said Ritchie Lee.

"There are places on the earth where no one has ever set foot," said Lugo. "The same is true of the insides of a house. No one ever walks closer than a foot or so from any wall without good reason." He reached out, grabbed Ritchie Lee by the upper arm, and pulled him next to the wallboard. "Ever find yourself standing here? I think not. Even when a person straightens a picture, they do it from a foot away."

Alison moved herself close to the wall, brushing it with a shoulder, to understand what Lugo was saying, and raised her eyebrows approvingly at Ritchie Lee who smiled back, even as he was thinking.

*

Ritchie Lee awoke before dawn and stepped about quietly. When Alison opened her eyes and realized he was not to be found anywhere inside the house, she concluded that he must have a very early delivery of water, until she looked out a window and saw the pickup was gone. Then she figured she must have misread his reaction to Miguel Lugo and that he was up at first light to find himself a router and a table saw so that he might begin work on her shelves before the cabinetmaker could even present her with a quote. *Well so be it,* she thought. *If he wants to build them, I should stop interfering.* She washed, dressed, dabbed perfume behind her ears, and left for the law offices in Lexington. About five miles up the parkway and beyond the lane closing, she flew her car over a rise and whizzed past the pickup on the side of the road. She slowed as fast as she could and pulled onto the shoulder about five hundred feet ahead. When traffic behind her was momentarily nowhere in sight, she gunned the car in reverse and backed along the shoulder to the truck. She thought maybe he was having engine trouble, or that the truck had run out of gas. Or maybe he'd had just too much coffee.

Ritchie Lee saw Alison get out of her car and walk to the pickup. He stood bent over in the middle of dozens of small cedars in a narrow gully below grade and five feet from the wire fence that marked the boundary of the parkway. The puzzlement on her face as she looked down at him was obvious. He waved her away, several times. Waved her to ignore him. To get herself to Lexington and the office. To just leave him be.

Reluctantly, Alison obeyed, although not immediately, and without ever saying a word she left, thinking she would find out after work what this was about. Then, as she sped off up the parkway and disappeared over the horizon, Ritchie Lee bent himself over further and spread apart the many small cedars here and there so that he might better see the ground beneath.

Except for the jogging, he knew that he would have done anything for her, if she had only given him the chance. This, now, was the least he could do, to visit this long narrow strip of land that went unnoticed and unvisited by everyday people, especially where heavy brush and foliage and out-of-sight ravines might hide a thing of interest. And while it crossed his mind that his actions would likely appear foolish to those same people, he couldn't help but wonder if Miguel Lugo's visit had been an answer to his prayer; and so ignoring the doubt, he promised he would look for Carly's body up and down the parkway all day if necessary, and tomorrow too.

DEAD TREE, DYING TREE

It wasn't until their fourth week on the property, after the moving was completed, the first of two weeks' vacation for Lisa had ended and she was back at work, and he had the outbuilding well on its way to becoming a functional studio, that he heard the cry. He was standing under the overhang of the back porch, admiring the unbroken view of rolling landscape turning green and pleased to no end they were out of the city and now owned a piece of land with acreage and quiet, when the wind picked up and began to agitate. The cry struck him as the kind that comes from determination faced with impending exhaustion, and at first he thought it was originating behind him, inside the farmhouse. But when he opened the door expecting the volume to increase, he realized that was not the case.

When Lisa returned in the evening, storm clouds were scudding overhead and the cry had not abated. He took hold of her arm and escorted her to the back porch.

"Listen," he said.

"What is that, Hollis? It's like the moaning of someone pinned beneath a collapsed building after an earthquake or an explosion. I hope it's temporary. I don't want to be forced to hear that all the time."

"I like it," he said, and he motioned her to follow. He led her to a pair of tall trees that had staked their claim next to a fence line overgrown with weeds, about two hundred feet north of the house. Their trunks were straight, thick with age, and no more than a few slivers of light flowed between. Barbed and woven wire were embedded inches deep beneath the bark in the one to the left.

"Look close," he said, "and let your eye move toward their crowns."

She did as suggested and nodded when she saw what he wanted her to see. Where the trunks' diameters narrowed, a pair of thick limbs was intertwined in a helix and each was moving against the other ever so slightly. The cry they produced on the wind was what Hollis and Lisa were hearing.

"And you like the sound," she said with a trace of incredulity.

"Because of what's going on. It's a cry of effort. It's kind of like they've been battling for the same small space year in and year out, and neither one is willing to give in," said Hollis. "And yet in another way they appear to be supporting each other."

"Don't you think one is eventually going to win out?"

"I don't know," Hollis said curiously, and she could see that he was, in fact, thinking about her question.

"What kind of trees are they? Do you know?"

"The one on the right is a hickory. The other a black walnut."

"And you're not supposed to plant a tomato plant next to a black walnut. Have you heard that?"

"I have. They release a chemical in the soil that is deadly to tomatoes and some other things. If we ever put in a garden, we'll need to remember that."

Moving out of the city and into the country had been Hollis's idea and he pushed Lisa to it with reasons that were real and financially sound, but the most motivating of them he had kept to himself. It was true that renting a studio had been an extra and somewhat exorbitant expense of which he wanted to be free, especially during those periods when photographic assignments suddenly became sparse; and it was equally true they had not the

56

money to purchase a larger house inside the city or out in one of its many burgeoning suburbs where prices made potential buyers wonder what the homes' current owners did for a living, and if all the jobs were even legal. But more than anything he had worried that Lisa was becoming too comfortable with the rat race so prevalent amid a populated area. And riding on that feeling was another he often experienced that suggested she was trying to draw him into it with all its craziness. Why had she thought even once that he would want to hear about Ken Dokes and Dana Crossley, two fellow employees who never did a lick of work and were apparently more than a little fond of each other, despite both were married with families? They sounded to him like a couple of first-class losers without skills and a work ethic, who were good neither in the closet nor out of it. And why had she pelted him with horrible stories about her supervisor Ross and that supervisor's superior Walt the Fault, an untidy and balding man whose fly was forever open at the top? The rip-and-rap had been daily, seemingly ongoing, it ran through weekends, and when she hadn't targeted his ear directly, he listened to it while she talked on the phone for hours with another employee who shared her feelings. The few times it appeared to be letting up and he would be afforded a respite, a neighbor from next door or across the street would venture over and the conversation began all over, with an additional litany of complaints coming from the neighbor who was suffering similarly at her own place of employment.

Lisa hadn't liked it when one evening, a month before they closed on the house, he accused her of reveling in the very things she was complaining about. "You get off on it," he said.

"Your problem," she answered, "is you're always stopping to smell the roses, and that isn't the real world, Hollis. It's not even close."

Not so! Too many questionable men and women peopled the world, he didn't doubt that for a second; and a great many of them were making more money, much more, than he would in a lifetime. But was it truly the real world? Not in his book. In his book the real world meant you took time to smell the roses.

Unfortunately, there were no rose bushes thriving on the new premises, but there was honeysuckle draping much of the fence line, plus lilac bushes and countless locust trees; and when they flourished into blossom, their fragrances filling the air and enveloping the farmhouse, he had his nose into them three and four times a day. He hoped to see Lisa do the same, hoped she would stop on the walkway en route to the car during those first mornings and inhale deeply the sweetness of each, but unless he suggested it, she made straight for the vehicle, shaking the key ring already in hand, a sign that she wasn't waiting to develop her battle plan for the day, that he and their little Yorkie were already out of mind, despite not yet out of sight.

It was pleasant on the farm day in and day out, just as he had expected, and although he had lost familiar customers because of the added distance to the new studio, Hollis worked hard and quickly to gain others. He especially enjoyed the studio work now because it allowed him to step outside anytime into the open air and feel only the breeze and hear only the birds. Or he would call for the Yorkie and together they would walk the property, the tiny dog appearing so out of place to Hollis amid both forest and open field.

In the beginning, in spite of her olfactory reluctance, Lisa did appear to respond to the bucolic nature of their new homestead and some of its palliative powers. Arriving home from work during those early months following the move, she still would talk of her day and lambaste her superiors along with several fellow employees, but Hollis observed that her treatment of it all was tempered and of lesser duration. It was not a problem for him to listen and remain attentive. On occasion he would even ask a question, like "Why does Dokes believe he should receive a promotion when he knows everyone regards him as lazy and incompetent?" Or "Why doesn't someone just come out and tell Walt the Fault to zip up?"

But during the autumn of their third year at their country

home, as they sat in the shade of the covered back porch enjoying a drink, Hollis noticed those same powers to soothe were disappearing.

"You don't hear it anymore, do you?" he remarked to her, a touch of sadness and defeat in his voice.

And the truth was she didn't. She had not heard even his question, and the cry of the intertwining trees which she once implied would drive her insane did not make the smallest dent in her present psyche. It was Dana Crossley on her mind.

"Sixty-five thousand dollars a year, plus an expense account, and the lazy ass can't make a monthly meeting! What's more, when he does show up, there's nothing that comes out of his mouth that's even remotely constructive."

It worsened with the following year and the one after that, as new names were added to the standbys, plus there were fresh conspiracies under examination and foul words uttered condemning the machinations hatched at the top of the corporate line. *Thank heavens*, Hollis muttered to himself, there weren't neighbors close by in the country who might visit on a regular basis to commiserate with her, but *Aha!* was he likewise to mutter in an effort to maintain his good humor, as Lisa, to his surprise, began inviting fellow employees to the farmhouse on weekends.

On those occasions, he could stand their double-barreled carping only so long before he vanished to the studio. Yet in a short while, the door opened and in would saunter Lisa and her "guest," usually each with a drink in hand, and he would be subjected to how the studio and himself, with his photographic abilities, could be co-opted to further punish, ridicule, or enlighten their many targets. *If only they knew,* he thought. Two of his last three commissions, he was bound to admit, were disappointments! And not just to the people who had commissioned them. They were disappointments to him as well.

He blew up. And finally he gave up.

It was a summer evening and she was on the phone. He was unable to determine who was on the other end. But the conversation was all too familiar, and he raised his voice, then took the phone away from her and slammed it back into its cradle.

"What the hell..." was all she said before she followed him outside.

There was a stiff breeze agitating the air, and it occurred to Hollis that the two interlocked trees weren't making their familiar sound. He walked out to them, the first time he had done so in a long time, and he saw immediately the hickory was dead. There wasn't a single leaf on it, and its contribution to the helix had been snapped off during some instance of foul weather. Holes dotted its shaggy bark, and he noticed a black slash where lightning had struck.

"Looks like the black walnut is the victor," declared Lisa.

He hadn't realized she had stolen up behind him. He turned to look at her, expecting anger, but there wasn't any.

"The walnut wins. Remember when you first showed me these trees? We hadn't been here very long. I asked which one you thought would ultimately win out."

"Which one did I pick? I don't recall."

"You didn't pick either, Hollis. But I did at the time, even though I never said so."

"And you went for the black walnut," he said. "Why was that?"

"I figured if it can kill tomato plants, how good is it for anything that it comes in contact with?"

Hollis nodded, but it wasn't a nod of agreement.

"I'm going back inside and fix myself a drink," said Lisa. "Would you like one?"

"Sure," said Hollis, who moved to the other side of the walnut tree as she walked back toward the farmhouse. The upper reaches on the north side of the tree showed a couple of limbs bare of leaves and many other branches with curled leaves of a sickly yellow hue. Near the base of the trunk, there was a hole and when he looked closely, he could see soft lichen was growing abundantly at ease inside the black walnut's wall.

He arched his head back and again stared up at the two trees, the one dead and the other that was obviously dying. And he realized the pair of trees had not been supporting each other all those years. Neither had their challenge been so noble as he had wanted to think. The cries and moans that had come with the wind were not strains born of effort and determination, but were merely the sounds of friction. Friction made by two living organisms, each just grinding against the other.

A BIGGER CASE

The black motorcycle with the double white pinstripe leaned on its side stand with the front wheel, headlight, and fairing angled longingly, almost pensively, to the left because Rip thought that was the pose at which all bikes look their best. He had bought the reliable BMW nearly fifteen years earlier from a middle-aged physician, who permanently garaged it before its first oil change following a deathly close call with a semi, and since then Rip had ridden aboard it through forty-nine of the fifty states and most of the Canadian provinces. Whenever the bike was parked and strangers gazed at it, he noticed how they soon checked the odometer, and they were always impressed by the mileage.

"Did you put all these on her?" they would ask, pointing to the numbers.

"Just about," Rip would answer with a solemn nod, never mentioning the more impressive fact that they had rolled over. "The two of us have been to quite a few places, and I've seen some beautiful sites."

Currently the mileage on the bike was pushing 200,000. Rip occasionally concluded it might be nearing twice that for himself, were it not for the tendency to live in cold environments. Why he didn't move from a snowy clime to the Sun Belt where a person could ride year-round, he wasn't sure. But the repeating process of moving from one job and rented living space to another was not a random one. He was, and continued to be, its director, although some family members, he was acutely aware, would never be disabused of their notion that he was shiftless and irresponsible.

The process had begun soon after graduating from college with a liberal arts degree and acquiring the bike. The desire to climb the ladder of any job simply held no interest for him.

"No interest?" an uncle started to expostulate at a family gathering. "What has that to do with eating everyday and putting a roof over your head?"

"I'll end up working as much as you do, Unc. Only when I

feel like hitting the pavement aboard the bike and exploring some new terrain, I won't be worrying myself stupid about surrendering up a job."

"That's because the jobs you're hired for won't be worth much!"

"That's what I mean," said Rip.

"I don't get it," the uncle said. "How do you intend to buy yourself a decent car and keep it insured? How are you going to save enough money for a down payment on a house? What if you knock some woman up?"

"No car, no house, no wife," Rip had said. "At least not for the next ten or twenty years. I plan on keeping no more belongings than I can pack into one or two cases. And absent a wife, I can head on up the road whenever the urge beckons."

While looking at the bike, he took a soft cloth and a special spray cleaner from a bucket sitting on a stoop in front of the old blue trailer, his current residence which displayed a crinkled panel near the tongue, and removed the smashed insects with their dried yellow enzymes decorating the fairing. When it came to *Show or Go*, he was definitely the latter. But some clean-up was an okay thing, too.

His uncle to this day remained unconvinced, and Rip, on the infrequent occasions he saw him, no longer insisted on making any effort to change his, or anyone's, mind. The truth was this: what he had intended is what came to pass. Money for a down payment on a home? Not a problem. He'd stashed away enough through the years to buy a small one or two bedroom house with outright cash when the time was right. An automobile? He never wanted one, and only once was he forced to buy a vehicle with four wheels when, after taking a job, he could not find either living quarters within walking distance or public transportation. And the warning about impregnating a woman did not foresee that he would become a practiced onanist, giving his lovers their satisfaction before he warmed the fuzzy tops of their tummies with a little of himself. Call him a true control freak. At least it was Rip Foley he was busy controlling, not unsuspecting others.

Yet, despite the plan unfolding as well as it had, a complete success it was not. With prosperous North America surrounding him, it was no matter Rip tried to deny himself material items because fate or some other invisible force insisted that he retain a few and not turn into a total ascetic. These possessions comprised mostly books, writings, photographic negatives and prints. Their accumulation connected to the jobs he worked for local promotional firms, weekly newspapers and pennysavers, regional magazines, and the like. He could write engaging copy, and he had the eye and knowledge to capture good photographs that were always of interest to others, and he was extremely efficient in the development and printing of these pictures. No matter where he moved, he always was able to talk the owners of these small businesses into accepting his help, and not a one would express anything but regret when he informed them that he was leaving to do some traveling. None of these creations and related materials did he want to throw out, but neither could he pack them along on a motorcycle. Fortunately, he developed friendships wherever he lived and when he spoke of his problem, there came, "Put the stuff in my basement," "Leave it in my garage," "We've a bedroom we never use, you can hide it there in a corner or under the bed," "Store it all in our attic, there's ventilation," "Dump it in the barn."

And that's what he had done in the previous years. In cities and towns in Pennsylvania, New York, Vermont, Maine, Quebec and elsewhere, there were things that belonged to Rip Foley.

He rubbed the final bug remains from the bike's upper fairing just as the postman arrived with a letter from his mother. She was cleaning house, she wrote, and was getting rid of everything upstairs and downstairs, in the garage too, that had not been touched for a decade, and this included several boxes of possessions belonging to her son.

"I'm going to set them out with the garbage, Rip, if I don't hear from you. And soon!"

The second message came only minutes later in a phone call

from a friend in Montreal with whom he had stayed a few years back. He was moving to new digs in a month. What did Rip want to do about the boxes of books, and no, he wasn't intending to ship them, there were too many and he was experiencing back pain.

And the last message Darcy delivered, as she was permitted to read his web-mail on her work computer because he didn't own one. She pulled her van in next to the trailer as he was returning to the outside stoop where it was cooler. He patted a spot for her beside him.

"Whatcha got?" he asked, seeing the sheet of paper in her hand.

"It's an e-mail from a friend of yours. The penis enlargement solicitations I threw in the trash. Or did you want them?"

Rip took the paper from her, smiling, and read its contents aloud: "*'We've had a fire and some of your things are ruined. You need to come get the rest of the boxes as soon as you can....Jeremy.'* Yeah, that's an old buddy from down Pennsylvania way."

He started laughing.

"What's so funny?" Darcy asked, already laughing a little herself and wondering what was funny about a house fire.

"Must be the Fates are at work. Can you believe it? This is the third message I've received in the last ten minutes, wanting me to come and collect my things. The first was from my mother. She's eager to toss, I know her pretty well. In fact, I think I better give her a call right now."

Darcy got up and followed him inside the trailer where he sat down at the kitchen table and dialed his mother's long-distance number. She was a tiny, freckled thing, about a foot shorter than he was. She began to rub his shoulders at the same time she brushed her nipples against his back.

"Hello, Mom? It's Rip. I just got your letter. Why do you feel like you have to throw out my things? What are they hurting where they are?"

"You need a house," his mother barked, ignoring his question.

"Aren't there any houses for sale in Ithaca?"

"Most mothers would say you need a wife," Darcy whispered to him after overhearing the words from Mrs. Foley seep from the telephone receiver.

"Can't you hold onto them a while longer? I'll be down real soon, I promise."

They went back outside after the call was ended. He sat back down on the stoop while Darcy threw a leg over the motorcycle. She started making acceleration and shifting sounds.

"Too loud," he said. "Beemers are quiet running, you know that. You want a beer or something?"

"No thanks. What's in these boxes that you have stored at various people's places?" she asked.

"Some things I've written. Photo stuff. My contact prints. Some finished prints as well. Assorted other things, like a toenail clipper and an old Zippo lighter from my smoking days. Maybe even a stale Oreo."

"You don't think you want to part with any of it?"

"Maybe after I look at it."

"So what's your plan?"

"Wish I had one."

"Then how about this. Since you don't want to take me with you on a bike trip—"

"You'd have to quit your secretarial job at the university, I told you that. When I go, I go with the intention of parking my carcass in some place new and different."

"Let me finish. What if I take you on one? We use my van. Go from one place to the next and collect all your things, all those mysterious boxes. I have two weeks vacation coming and they start next week."

"What about me?"

"What about you? Quit. That's what you just said you normally do."

"I'm not ready to quit this job just yet," he said while his eyes narrowed in capricious thought. "But, I probably can talk my way into some time off."

"All right then, Big Boy! We'll leave on Monday."

"Holster your gun, Darce. What am I supposed to do with these boxes once we get them back here? I'm cramped in this crappy trailer as is."

"Well don't look at me. My apartment isn't any better. Have you considered renting a small storage compartment?"

"I don't need the expense."

"They're not that much."

"They're enough. Even so, what happens when I do make my exit?"

"Stop worrying about it for now. When you get them all back here, something will come to mind. Maybe even a bonfire."

*

They departed Ithaca early Monday, soaring up over the hill and past the gorgeously groomed campus of Cornell University. The morning was already a perfect summer one with blue sky, and fresh fragrances were filling the air. Montreal would be their first destination.

"Are you all right?" asked Darcy.

"Sure. What's on your mind?"

"I just mean, you know, that you usually travel alone and on your bike."

"Hey, we're going to have fun," he said. "Are you willing to let me drive this thing?"

"Would you allow me to drive the Beemer?"

"Nooo."

"Well then…."

He knew she wasn't serious.

"Before we go much further, let's stop somewhere and get us a box of donuts and a couple of cappuchinos," he said. "My sweet tooth is acting up."

They made Montreal by nightfall in drizzling rain. Rip called his friend to tell him they would be by in the morning to pick up his boxes containing the books and other possessions, but there was no answer and he wasn't able to leave a message.

"I hope he's there tomorrow and not at work. I don't want to stick around all day waiting."

Because it was wet outside, they ignored erecting the biker's tent that Rip had brought along and instead slept in the van, hugging each other most of the night. In the morning they drove to his friend's apartment located in a small complex outside the city. As soon as his friend appeared at the door, Rip knew the back injury was understated and that it was probably the reason the phone had gone unanswered.

"Gawd, you look terrible," said Rip. "What happened?"

"It went out on me lifting a couple of beer cases into the cooler. I've been off work already four weeks, which is why I figured maybe I should get a cheaper place to live. I've the feeling this is going to be more trouble than I'd like."

"Sorry, Ace," said Rip, and then he introduced Darcy.

"There's your stuff," his friend said, after nodding at Darcy, and pointed to a corner behind the door.

"I thought you said you wouldn't be moving for a month."

"Right. But I knew you'd be coming around as soon as possible, so I got someone to haul them from the back room to here. They were getting in my way. You get yourself screwed up like this and everything gets in your way."

Rip grinned to cover his annoyance, but all the same he voiced the question: "What the hell made you think I would be coming up so soon?"

The friend opened his eyes like he couldn't believe the question needed asking. "You're ready, Rip," he said. "You've been ready." And then he laughed with pain and looked over at Darcy. "Can you two stay awhile? Can I get you something?"

"No," said Rip. "We're on kind of a whirlwind tour. Besides, did I say you look like hell? You best stay put and rest up."

From there they traveled back into the States, where Customs wanted a close look at the insides of the boxes, then rolled down to the very southern part of Maine. So long as he was bent on doing this, he might as well collect everything, he told Darcy, except for some things stashed with people when he had freelanced out west. The friend in Maine was a sexy older woman with whom he had worked at the newspaper that covered Kennebunkport and areas below along the shore.

Rip lugged up two boxes from the basement of her house, one a large original container for Girl Scout cookies.

"This is the first they moved since you left them. So everything should be inside, except that if any of it was edible, the mice may have destroyed it. They've given me fits at times. In fact, a hundred miles from here the pair of you might discover you've got a stowaway. You're looking good, Rip."

Darcy thought the woman was looking awfully good herself, despite her age, and there was something about how the woman emphasized the word "edible" that bothered her. She was happy when Rip said goodbye.

They enjoyed a scrumptious, freshly caught fish dinner at a shack-like restaurant on the beach, and then it was on to Vermont and a husband and wife. His stuff was gone, they told him apologetically. The husband was embarrassed.

"What do you mean 'gone'? Did someone steal it?"

The husband swung his eyes over to his wife.

"I'm sorry, Rip," she said. "When I looked inside, I thought it was old belongings of ours."

"Was there only one box?"

"Yes," said the wife.

"By the time I realized it was your things, Rip, it was too late. Penny included it as part of her yard sale and it went quickly."

"I received about twenty dollars for it. Let me get you the money."

"Forget it, Penny," Rip said. "Consider it a storage fee. Do you remember what was inside?"

"A couple of old LPs and an early CD or two, all of them scratched up. A photo album without photos, just some picture postcards that were never used. I forget what else."

Back in the van, Rip said to Darcy, "If I myself have no inkling what I left with them, it must not be worth too much."

"Where to?" asked Darcy with a map open before her.

"Back into New York for one stop at Lake George, then we'll take 'er down to Pennsylvania for stops at Jeremy's and my Mom's."

The friend at Lake George was away on business with his wife, but a teenage son was home in charge and permitted him to search through the attic of the house and locate his things while the boy himself kept stealing glances at Darcy's perky breasts. From there Rip got behind the wheel and drove the entire route into southeastern Pennsylvania and the farm belonging to his friend Jeremy.

It was another understatement they found the following morning. More than half the farmhouse had been destroyed in the fire, and Rip wondered how much of his own stuff did remain. The friend Jeremy appeared out of the barn when they arrived. There was no enthusiasm from either man, and the reunion was somber. Jeremy's wife came out of the damaged house, but never made an effort to learn who had driven up to the property. To Rip it meant the fire must somehow have been the fault of his lanky friend and so he refrained from asking the obvious question.

It was otherwise with Darcy. "What happened?" she said as she stared at the blackened structure.

"Not sure," said Jeremy. "Fire Marshal was here and thinks it might have been electrical."

"How are you doing?" Rip managed to ask.

"I don't know," said Jeremy. "Sometimes I think you've had the right idea all along. Reduce everything you own down to what will fit on a motorcycle."

Rip said nothing in reply.

"What's left of your things are in the barn. I moved them, along with most of ours. We're able to sleep in the one room and the kitchen is still somewhat usable, plus the computer survived.

71

But beyond that everything is burned or water-damaged."

"I'm sorry," Rip said. "Any way I can help?"

Jeremy shook his head.

"Well look then. Darcy and I aren't going to hang around. We'll just load the things into the van and be on our way. But if you need anything or you think I can help, let me know. I still intend to be in upstate New York for awhile."

From there they turnpiked to his mother's home, Darcy driving most of the two hundred miles. It was already into evening when they pulled into Mrs. Foley's driveway. Darcy knew she was showing some excitement about meeting Rip's mother, but she noticed that he wasn't in any way encouraging it, and she understood the reason soon enough. Mrs. Foley's interest continued to be along the lines that her boy should buy himself a house. She barely looked at Darcy, even during introductions, and never smiled or said a word in her direction.

"I'm going back outside and sit in the van," said Darcy. "If you were thinking of staying here, forget it. Or if you're dead set on it, I'll get a room somewhere and pick you up in the morning."

"She's always like that. It doesn't have a thing to do with you."

"Well, there's the problem. I'd like her to have something to do with me."

"Don't go. I'll load up, then make an excuse. We'll find us a nice room tonight where we can shower and all."

There were six boxes, a couple of some size, and he had to drag all of them from underneath the garage rafters and onto the concrete floor. Once they were in the van, it was clear to them both that sleeping inside the vehicle would no longer be an option.

Mrs. Foley came outside.

"Give me a minute," Rip said to Darcy.

"Did you find them all? There were six."

"I got them all," Rip said, then he placed a hand alongside each shoulder of the testy woman and held her straight. "Mom, you know we'd like to stay and visit with you, but we really can't. We got to head on back. I'll write or give you a call in the next couple of weeks, okay?"

"You sure you didn't miss one? 'Cause if you did, I'm just going to throw it out. I hate having junk around."

"I got them all, Mom. We'll see you, all right?"

He kissed her on the cheek, then climbed into the van. Without hesitation or any farewell of her own, Darcy backed the vehicle out of the driveway. Before the transmission was shifted out of reverse, Mrs. Foley had turned away and was headed back to her front door.

"Seems there were seven boxes," Darcy remarked to herself.

"What's that?"

"Let's travel out of this area before we look for a motel."

"Sounds good to me," said Rip. "Do you know where you're heading?"

"Directions will help, seeing that it's your old stomping grounds we're in."

*

Most of the first week of Darcy's vacation was gone since their departure from Ithaca, and the driving had taken its toll on each. They found a Hampton Inn for the night and luxuriated in the shower. In the morning they slept late, and neither was in a hurry once on their feet, as both knew they had accomplished the mission with time to spare. Although they were but a day's ride from home, they also had another week to play.

"Ever hear of the Kinzua Bridge?" Rip asked. "It's a magnificent structure made of wood and iron, and very old. It was a bridge for trains. It's now a state park with camping facilities. We're about three hours from it."

Darcy thought Rip would want to drive them to the old bridge, but instead he told her to get behind the wheel because he wanted to have a look at the contents of the some of the boxes.

The first thing he removed from them was a stack of exposed photographic paper.

"Contact prints?" asked Darcy, glancing from the highway.

Rip turned them over and looked at his file numbers crayoned in the corner. "Early ones."

The stack was thick and Darcy guessed there were at least three-hundred of the prints showing the actual size of all the pictures on the all the rolls he had shot during those years.

"And there's more?"

"Should be in some of the other boxes."

"But none of those are of any use if there aren't negatives, are they?"

"Those should be there too, each in its own glassine. Hopefully, there weren't any in the box Penny sold at her yard sale. I wonder about the fire, too."

Suddenly, an odd thought occurred to Darcy as she was again glancing at him and the stack of contact prints.

"Do you even own a camera?" she asked. "I mean it, Rip! I can't recall ever seeing one sitting out anywhere in your trailer."

"I used to own one, until it was stolen along with a few lenses and my expensive strobe. After that, I started using the equipment of the people for whom I worked."

"You can get a job like that? Tell them you'll shoot pictures, but you don't have a camera?"

Rip laughed. "No. For starters, they look at me the same way you're looking at me. But once I show them some of the things I've done, the first hook is in. That's because I do very good work. The second hook then gets me the job. I tell them if I use their equipment, I charge less. In many cases, a lot less. Some of these people relish the idea that someone besides themselves will use their camera and equipment. Many can't stand going out to shoot pictures and they often wonder why they purchased the camera in the first place, not to mention processing paraphernalia, which they hate working with even more. My plan settles their anxiety about spending hundreds of dollars on photo equipment. I put it to good use. What's more, I make it a habit of always bringing the camera back to the office or shop when I'm done, in case the boss or someone on the staff wants to put it to use. That's why you don't see one hanging about in the trailer."

Darcy covered the highway distance eagerly and the van was soon rolling through the mountains. At the peak of one, at the end of a small town with the name Mt. Jewett, Rip told her to make a left and follow the road for about five miles whereupon they would likely find a sign directing them where to turn to reach the bridge and campground.

The bridge was spectacular, Darby exclaimed upon seeing it, and they quickly picked out a campsite, as there were no other visitors, and set up the tent. Afterwards, she wanted them to walk over to the bridge. It was a massive structure, still black all over with its thousands of creosoted timbers and the iron framework beneath. It stretched across a long valley, perhaps three hundred feet in the air at the deepest point, and there was nothing to be seen all around except dense forest in full summer foliage.

A chain was stretched across the start of the bridge with a sign attached forbidding visitors to walk across the rail bed because severe rot had been identified in many of the timbers. As no one was around, they both ignored the sign, but still they did not advance very far. Darcy said she only wanted to peer down from the top, and so after about thirty paces, they turned back, choosing next to hike the ground underneath the bridge and among the framework, whose great supports resembled a diminishing succession of A's. When they trudged back to the tent more than an hour later, Rip told her he was going to lie down awhile because he suddenly felt tired. Darcy declined his offer to do the same. Instead, she took the magazine purchased during their previous stop and went to sit quietly at a picnic table.

The two bikes with their leather-clad riders glided into the campground and past her before she knew it. Both were Beemers, she realized once she looked up, a dark blue one fully decked and a white in-line that appeared equally equipped. When the helmets came off, Darcy could see that each couple was older than she and Rip, who could be heard gently snoring inside the tent.

The women, with their hair pinned on top their heads, smiled at her, and Darcy closed the magazine and walked over to the riders to say hello.

"Been out on the bridge?" the shorter of the men asked, removing a Nikon camera from a case on the white bike.

"It's rotted," answered Darcy. "They don't want anyone walking on it and falling through to their death. My boyfriend and I went out a ways just to get the feel of how high it is."

"Guess that means we'll just have to take a few pictures and let it stand as that," said the other man, who was rather handsome, Darcy thought.

"These are beautiful bikes," she said.

The shorter man said, "You ride?"

"Some. My boyfriend, who's asleep inside the tent—we've been on the go everyday this past week—he owns a Beemer, and he's been all over. The bike has almost two-hundred thousand miles on it and he's the one who traveled most of them."

"That's bragging mileage," said the handsome one, nodding.

One of the women said, "He doesn't take you with him on the long journeys, Sweetie?"

She didn't know why, but she felt it necessary to lie. "I can never get off work," Darcy answered the woman.

"You're off now," said the man with the Nikon. "Where's the Beemer?" When Darcy appeared confused, the man added, "I saw the New York plates on the van. Aren't you on some sort of trip?"

"Oh," said Darcy. "He left things behind in his travels and all the places he's worked, and we spent the past week collecting everything. My van is packed full with boxes containing his possessions. What he's going to do with all of it, I don't know. He doesn't either. My apartment is small and the mobile home that he rents…well, it's not much bigger."

The handsome one said, "Ask me, gathering his things together, he's getting ready to rein himself in some."

"Is that in your interest?" pried the woman who had spoken before.

She was smiling at Darcy, and Darcy smiled her best smile back. She would never deny that she wanted Rip to marry her. However, she disagreed that he was ready.

"I think he wants to continue to travel on the bike for a while and set down in other towns and work," she said. "That's what he's always enjoyed doing. Would you like me to wake him?"

"Let him rest," said the shorter one who was fumbling with the lens and knobs atop the camera. "It's a great day for it. We just wanted to see the bridge, then we're running up to the Pennsylvania Grand Canyon. They say it's beautiful."

The handsome biker said to Darcy, "He may want to keep on riding, Miss, but he'll also likely want to get himself a new machine. These cycles enjoy a reputation for long service, it's true, but the mileage you quoted still suggests a lot of wear and tear, and if he wants to do some more cross-country, I suspect he'll first do some shopping."

Rip had never made mention of looking for a new bike, but what the good-looking man said made sense to her. "Maybe after he sells the one he has," allowed Darcy.

"Or, more likely, he'll just get himself a bigger case," said the shorter one with the camera, which was now at eye level and focused on the two women. "You get in the picture, too," he ordered Darcy.

Darcy missed the drift of his comment as both women reached out and pulled her between them.

"He won't be selling his bike," murmured the first woman. "The men who own these Beemers, Sweetie, are reluctant to ever get rid of them."

"Especially when mileage and memories are attached," said the second woman. "Perish the thought."

"I've three besides the one we're on," said the handsome husband in confirmation. "Ray here owns two."

Chkkkk went the shutter. "Gotcha," Ray said. "What's your name?"

*

77

Rip told Darcy he was glad she hadn't awakened him. Not that he wouldn't have enjoyed meeting other BMW bike owners, but he preferred talking with them at some length over a couple of beers, which was why every year he attended two or three weekend state rallies.

The next morning he found her at the picnic table with the map spread out in front.

"Have you been to the Pennsylvania Grand Canyon?" she asked.

"I take it you haven't," he said.

"Is it beautiful?"

"It's real pretty. Peaceful, too." He nudged her to make room for himself beside her on the table's bench, and together they looked at the map. "I have an idea. Let's pick up a few groceries, then camp there tonight at the head. We'll rent a canoe, and in the morning paddle our way through the rapids and all the way down to—"

"Rapids! Rip, I've canoed, but I'm not someone you want to take down any dangerous rapids."

"The water's low this time of year," he said. "They won't be a problem. It'll take us most of the day to reach the end. Tomorrow evening we'll set up the tent at—"

"What about the van? How are we going to get back to my van?"

"Ah, the van," said Rip, having momentarily forgotten its presence. "Well, we'll just have to give a few bucks to a couple of local trustworthy hillbillies to drive it down to Aintry." And then pretending that he was one of those hillbillies, he exclaimed with utter disbelief, "AIN-tree!"

Darcy was suddenly lost with his behavior, plus she didn't see any Aintry on the map, and Rip had to explain that the hillbillies and the Georgia town were references to a favorite movie, *Deliverance*. "The actual town is…" and he put a strong finger on the Pennsylvania map, "…is Blackwell."

"Aintry *is* a much more interesting name," said Darcy, which spurred him to exclaim again in his exaggerated hillbilly voice, "AIN-tree!"

*

The creek running through the canyon was low, confirming Rip's prediction, and the stretch of rapids was absent of the exciting whitewater prevalent in early spring. Even so, they managed to steer the canoe into the famous big rocks at the first bend and almost capsized, relieved it was only their feet that underwent a soaking.

Toward evening they floated into Blackwell. Darcy was expecting a small town or hamlet. Instead, the enclosed area displayed just three wooden structures, none of which showed any signs of use for at least half a century.

"What's that in the van?" asked Darcy.

Rip went over and discovered that two cups of coffee, still warm, were sitting on the dash.

"Gee, that was nice of them to think of that," she said.

"I'll say," said Rip. "These will more than hit the spot." And he took one and handed the other to her.

"Darce, I know I said yesterday we could camp here tonight on the creek bank. But if you want, we can simply get in the van, return the canoe, then continue up the road."

"Either way," she answered.

"You have something on your mind?"

"I'm enjoying myself. And I'm doing it with you."

"So am I."

"Rip honey, are you thinking that one day you'll up and leave Ithaca for some place new?"

"That's what you're thinking about?"

"Some."

"It's what I usually do, you know that."

"Isn't the bike becoming too old for that sort of thing?"

"How's that?"

"For long-distance cross-country, I mean. Wouldn't it be

difficult to get a hold of parts if you were to break down miles away from nowhere?"

"I see what you're getting at. And, yes, I probably will have to look at a new machine one of these days very soon if I want to pick up and go again."

"Will you trade in the one you have?"

It was a trick question she was asking, but there was information from him she needed, and she was guessing that he would not immediately catch on, the same as she hadn't when the shorter biker from yesterday mentioned the phrase.

"Trade...? No way, Darce. I've too much of myself invested in the ol' Beemer to ever give it up."

"Then I suppose you'll just have to get yourself a bigger case," she said with a smile.

"A bigger case...? Yes, I suppose I will," he said, smiling back.

"Let's camp here tonight, get a fire going, and I'll make us something to eat," she said, but at the same time she was thinking to herself the house should have two floors with plenty of closet space, a nice wraparound porch, and two or three acres at least so their dogs could run.

Rip, standing on the bank and looking into the water, suddenly said, "It'll have to be a mighty big case, Darce, don't you think?"

A ROOT CELLAR MEMORY

How ironic it seems that my mother, who worked throughout her life with her mind, became afflicted with Parkinson's while my father, who's worked his entire life with his hands, suffers from Alzheimer's.

Before Janet's death she insisted I see the doctor to learn if I had it, Alzheimer's. She'd worried because she thought I was exhibiting signs, despite I wasn't 50. But the doctor cautiously agreed with her after running tests and capturing several pictures—slices—of my brain. He said my father also might have had the early form of it, except the disease wasn't much recognized in past generations as it is today. He was a tanned, in-shape physician with a Pete Sampras-inscribed tennis racket and a snowboard at the ready in the corner of his office. His advice included keeping my mind active. He asked if I read much, messed with puzzles, and did similar things that challenged the mind and demanded mental exercise. I answered that I still managed to slog through a dozen or so books every year, although my vision up close was beginning to show problems. I said also that when I was a younger man, I enjoyed writing short stories.

"Well, if that's so, Mr. M., then I recommend you do like the oilmen in this country are currently doing. Get that rusty pump working again, there's profit to be made. In your case, that translates to a longer quality of life. Making up a story insists on an attention to detail and chronology, doesn't it? So that's just what the disease often robs its victim of. Plus who knows," he added, laughing, "perhaps you'll win a Pushcart."

I intended to heed his advice, although I would not be sending out my stories (the early ones weren't really all that made-up anyway, if truth be told) to magazines for possible publication. Revising, rewriting, these were not things I'd done in the past, and they held no interest now. The fact was, once I'd completed a story, then assigned it a title, into an accordion folder the typewritten manuscript had gone with others. Already tired of it, I didn't read my words even to myself.

But before I could start, I was stopped. That's because my Janet was suddenly dead. Twenty-two years we were together with hardly a cruel word spoken, and we had hoped to be together for at least that same length of time again. But while shopping at the downtown stores in early February for a new comforter to keep us warm at night, a six thousand-pound slab of concrete dislodged from an aboveground municipal parking structure and killed her.

I quit my well paying but dead-end job (no reason I can see to mention it) and put the house up for sale after deciding to go and live with my father and look after him, as well as to help take my mind off the loss of my wife. A few years before her death, Janet, who could be compassionate to a fault, had suggested I bring him to live with us, only he wouldn't hear of leaving his home and the forty acres of woodland surrounding it. Now that I was alone and we had widower status in common, it seemed right to make the move. Although he hadn't appeared to worsen during recent visits, and he remained capable of taking adequate care of himself, all the same I knew it was just a matter of time until his condition deteriorated to the tipping point. And once that occurred, I knew, too, horrible things could happen.

*

I arrived here at the home of my upbringing in early June, a house sufficiently isolated, particularly so when the foliage was out, that other structures in the neighborhood were not visible from any of the four directions. My father welcomed me, literally, with open arms, and ordered me to park my car in the garage since it is a much newer model than his own. It was always a strength of his (and a strength I hope I've inherited, should my Alzheimer's—if the doctor and his tests are correct—progress) that he knew who and what were important to him, and who and what were not. Both sides of this coin remained unaffected by the disease. For example, eating had never held a special place for him in the events of any day. When my mother was alive and in control of her motions, he downed without remark or savor whatever she cooked and put on the table. After she became debilitated and especially after she was gone, he ate the contents of his cupboards and refrigerator without preference or discretion. Six pickles and a bold slice of cheddar were regarded the same as a plateful of galumpki. It was different with his drink. He knew at any moment the contents of the liquor cabinet, what he was low on, and what he might be in the mood for on the following day, and I found this had not changed. With people, he exercised himself in similar fashion. Never had he failed to recognize my mother or me, to call up countless memories of our family vacations to Wildwood and Ocean City, and he loved Janet so much that he could have told anyone asking, where his daughter-in-law had grown up and what her interests were. Yet he loathed his closest neighbor, and one of the earliest signs of the disease was that he forgot the man, name and all, along with his spouse.

One night several months after I had unpacked my suitcases in my old upstairs bedroom, a car drove up our lane. There was but a thin crescent of moon and a light snow was falling, nothing sticking. While I sat watching a Boston Pops holiday special, he sipped at his Drambuie and pushed around a few magazines on the coffee table. These were magazines without subscription that came in the mail from the gas and electric companies, and the "pushing around" of things was a new habit just beginning to form. He saw the car lights at the same time I did and glanced at the clock.

"Who do you think that is?" I asked.

"I don't know," he answered, and I wondered if he really didn't, or had he invited someone over whom he later forgot about, which he had done previously.

The house with its covered wraparound porch sat away from the end of the lane. The car came to a stop directly in front of the garage. I switched the porch light on and could see it was a much older car, one of those manufactured before the demand for better mileage. A huge rusting crater decorated the passenger side and a hubcap was missing from the rear wheel, which was one of those skinny, donut-like spares that were around for a time, a tire you weren't supposed to travel on at speeds faster than fifty. Two men got out and they looked to be in their early thirties. Both were of the same height, but one had an excess of cockiness to his walk. The other had a few pounds on the first, most of it seeming to hug the waistline. Both were stuffed inside dark, bulky canvas jackets like you see warming seamen in icy waters, and neither was wearing a thing on his head. They stepped onto the porch and knocked at the door. We'd never had a bell installed.

I started to open the door, but was prevented by my father's hand. It reached in front to quietly click the lock.

A second, louder knock sounded.

"You in there!"

"I'll be right with you," my father said in a calm voice.

He then raised a finger and waved it at me in a side-to-side motion.

"Aw, come on," said a second voice. "Open up." And then I heard a rattle of the storm door, but it was locked too.

My father, who had gone into his bedroom, returned in just seconds, and he didn't look any different. I worked my eyes at him as though to say "What's going on?" but he stepped to the side of me, unlocked the door, and opened it.

"Hey, we need some help," one of the visitors said through the storm door, and all I could see of him was his hand, which was on the latch, and the hand was dirty. I thought it probably belonged to the cocky one.

"What is it?" my father asked. His tone was friendly but cautious.

That's when I stepped out, which produced a rapid eye movement between the pair. Cocky wore a silver ring in his left ear and a tattoo of something I couldn't make out stretched down his neck and under his collar. His skin looked much less like a natural cover protecting the flesh that lay beneath and more like a husk, desiccated and shot through with crevice upon crevice. Meth user is what came to mind.

"Our cell phone's dead," the heavier one said, addressing me with his eyes, which were selling an affability the moment did not warrant.

I started to ask what was their problem, why they were in need of assistance since it appeared their car hadn't broken down, when my father cut me off.

"Why up here, off the road?" he asked.

"Hey, we tried other houses, old man. Didn't we, Robes? It's the Christmas season. People are shopping, what'd you think?" And without waiting for another reply from either of us, this one, the cocky bastard, must have become suspicious of my father's awareness and wrenched the storm door open with such enormous violence that it broke loose from its hinges.

Barely a second elapsed, it seemed, and they were inside the house, pressing guns in our faces. The cocky one shoved my father backward, shoved him hard, causing him to stumble and smash his leg on the coffee table.

I started to say "Take it easy," but never got all of it out as the other one swung the barrel of his gun across my face. I lurched to the floor bleeding. My jaw, I thought, must certainly be broken.

"Now you both shut your holes unless we ask a question," the cocky one said. "You don't? Well...." He pretended to fire his gun at each of our heads and said, "Bingo, bango."

My father was rubbing his leg. He righted himself and backed onto the sofa.

"You all right?" he said to me.

Blood was trickling out of my mouth and the bones circling it were reeling with pain, but I nodded anyway.

"Who the fuck are you?" The cocky one asked. "This beef jerky's supposed to be living alone."

"He's my father," I said.

"Yeah? Well, see that he behaves."

His partner had disappeared into the rear of the house, and now came some mumble from that direction, which made Cocky turn partly away from us, even though his gun continued to point in our direction. My father raised himself from the sofa, a silent movement so arresting of me because of its ageless grace that my mouth ceased hurting. And as he did, his right arm reached with equal grace behind his back to the lower spine where he withdrew a gun of his own, one of two he'd owned for as long as I can remember. This one was the .45, a semiautomatic he'd inherited from an uncle who had fought in the war in France and Germany. He glided the two steps to our closest invader and placed the .45 at the back of Cocky's head. In a calm whisper, while he took away Cocky's gun, he said, "Tell your friend to come out here. Tell him to drop his gun."

When Cocky hesitated, my father cocked his own, just like in the movies.

"ROBES!" Cocky shouted. "GET OUT HERE!"

My father beckoned me to hide, and I slipped onto the first stair leading to the second floor.

"What's up?" I heard Robes say, and it was clear by his tone a step or two remained before he would discover that circumstances were changed.

"Set it down," I heard my father order.

"Where's the other one?"

"Forget it, Robes! Do as he says."

Silence then, as Robes was thinking. Ten seconds might have passed. Finally, Robes's gun hit the floor, and I was summoned.

"I'll call the police," I said as I picked up the gun.

"We don't want to sit on guard," my father said hastily. "We might fall asleep."

"So what do you want to do then?"

"Find a flashlight, son. We'll take them out to the root cellar."

*

I'd helped my father build the root cellar when I was a boy. We dug out a shoulder-high knoll at the rear of the backyard, some two hundred feet from the house, then packed the inside wall with rock. To support the roof, a dome, my father interlaced several timbers he'd felled on the property. Afterwards, we rounded the top with soil so that this root cellar looked like a very large green tortoise, partially buried, once the grass reappeared. The door, too, became special. Not the original one, but the door that was hung a few years later and was on it to this day. Two thick slices of solid white oak with a Sargent padlock about half the size of my palm.

On the walk back to the house, I took the .45 from my father's hand.

"What's the matter?" he asked. "You don't trust me? Your mother didn't trust me with it either."

"Not the case, Dad. I just see you're favoring the leg. I don't want it to give out, and then maybe the gun accidentally goes off and one of us gets hurt."

He didn't respond to this, and I wanted to think it was because he knew my concern was an honest one. I was grateful that in the face of what had just happened and worse, what might have happened, he had remembered the gun, what it was for, and where to find it. It was, in a way, striking a blow against the Alzheimer's.

I shined the light on the grass in front of him so he could safely see where he was stepping.

"Dad, do you remember the Fantuzzis?"

"They were your mother's friends. I remember."

"No, they weren't Mom's friends. They were that family that lived in that rundown house at the end of Slidell Hollow. They had a passel of kids, remember? But that was about all they had. They moved out when I started high school."

"Thieves. They should have been hanged."

"Not really, Dad," I said, smiling in the dark. I was pretty sure he was thinking of another family from further on down the road. The Lomasters. The father and his three sons were notorious for stealing items right off a family's lawn and front porch. To this day I'm convinced it was the middle boy Dwight who took my J.C. Higgins, the only bike around with a speedometer.

He gave me that look that was supposed to assure me (but in fact and without his knowing, it did just the opposite—this simplest form of cover for the Alzheimer victim who's not yet surrendered completely to the disease) that he was extracting items from his memory, which was the reason I had brought up the Fantuzzis and numerous others in the months since arriving. Living alone, he'd had no one to stimulate his memory, and I wanted to serve in that role. It would be a beneficial thing for me as well, and if our recollections of an event were different, what would it matter, so long as his were not so far off the mark to suggest we were losing each other. I tried once more. This time narrowing the Fantuzzi field.

"What about little Guido? Do you remember him?"

I thought he might because Guido, along with his brothers and sisters—but Guido especially—was, in a way, the reason Dad had replaced the door on the root cellar. The Fantuzzis were poor, and so each autumn the children raided nearby cornfields, knowing ahead of time which rows were planted with the sweet ears. They descended on the orchards too, ripe with various fruits, and some of the neighborhood's more promising backyard gardens. This was their way of insuring the family got its dietary greens and daily nutriments. However, they never took more than what they felt was needed for sustenance, and never did they vandalize what was left behind. Some of the residents in their area of operation complained to the county sheriff, but the Fantuzzi family was early proof for me that being poor did not translate to being stupid.

Then one year the stealing escalated, and orchards were destroyed, gardens mutilated, and our root cellar broken into and everything ruined, including hundreds of canned fruits and vegetables put up by my mother. People again pointed a finger at the Fantuzzis, explaining that the shift from theft alone to theft with vandalism was because they had left childhood and were en route to their teens.

Dad and I were cleaning up the mess when Guido showed up.

"I didn't do this, sir. My brothers and sisters didn't have anything to do with it either."

"I know that, Guido."

88

"I mean it, sir. We didn't do this. We haven't done any of this around here that people are saying we did. We wouldn't do this kind of thing."

"I know, Guido. I believe you," Dad said.

"You do?" The expression on Guido was one of surprise. He must have thought my father would call him a liar.

"Sure. You're a nice kid. And so are your brothers and sisters. You want to help my boy and me clean up this mess? We could use the help. You show up tomorrow, too, Guido. I've got a surprise for you."

The next day Guido and I helped my father to hang the new oak door with the big padlock. When it was done, my father reached into a pocket, pulled out two keys on a ring, and removed one. This he gave to Guido.

"You're in charge, Guido. You and any of your brothers and sisters can walk in here whenever your family wants some fruits or vegetables. Or if you just have a craving for an apple and it's that time of year when there aren't any on the trees."

Anyway, I asked Dad a second time if he remembered little Guido Fantuzzi, but he said he didn't know any Guido, and we went back inside the house where I set the guns of our intruders on top of the refrigerator.

"Where do you want yours?" I then asked him.

He took the .45 from my hand and went back inside the living room to finish his drink. The television was still on, but the Pops Christmas concert had finished. He placed the gun on the table with the magazines. As I picked up the phone, I started to say that he should unload the thing, but then thought better of it. There wasn't much chance the home invaders would break out of the root cellar, but if they did, it seemed wise to keep the gun loaded and ready to fire.

How could he not have a single recollection of the smallest Fantuzzi! I asked myself. I just couldn't believe that he had forgotten little Guido so completely! It was my father's words that day inside the root cellar that were responsible for the self-esteem I saw in Guido in the remaining years before his family moved west. I put the phone back in its cradle—I'd already forgotten why I'd picked it up. But I told myself then and before going to bed that night, I told myself I would bring up Guido again the following day.

*

The next morning when I came downstairs, he was fixing himself a bowl of cereal.

"We got hunters," he said.

I looked out a window at a beat-up car parked squarely in front of the garage. Most times the hunters would stop, walk up to the house and ask permission, but down the years there had been some, strangers, who just drove up, got out, and disappeared to the back of our land. There were times even when they'd blocked in my mother from getting out to work, and we had to move their car into the field on either side. That was going to be the case this morning if these trespassers didn't show up soon, because I needed to go to the store for several items, and I would move their car with my own if forced to.

But for now, I put some water on the stove for instant coffee and went to sit in the other room. One of my father's two guns was there on the table.

"Dad? Why's your .45 out?"

"That must be your mother's doing," I heard him say from the kitchen. "You know she doesn't like having guns around. She wants to throw it out."

I shook my head—before coming, I'd warned myself not to be overly dismayed by the occasionally serious lapse—and then remembered that yesterday, or maybe the day before, I had asked him if he remembered the Lomasters. Old man Lomaster and his sons were people you always had to be on the lookout for, because they would steal a person blind, steal things right off your front lawn and porch with you in the house. To this day I'm convinced it was the middle boy Dwight who took my J.C. Higgins, the only

90

bike in our part of the township with a speedometer. And Dad was convinced they would try for his car next! This, I figured, was probably the real reason for the gun's appearance, even though Lomaster himself is dead and his sons live elsewhere.

And then I thought, *Check to see if he's loaded it.*

I released the clip into my other hand. Two cartridges had been jammed in, above the spring. Each angled so it would not fall out. Each too small for the weapon. Each a .22, the caliber of his second gun.

He appeared out of the kitchen with his bowl of cereal. Some milk had dribbled from his mouth and was beading at the corner. Up till then I had not felt sorry for my father. But I now knew he was a danger to not just himself, but to others as well. I realized he would require watching more closely, and that I would have to take preventive measures. The first of these included hiding the gun from him. I would have to keep it myself.

"What happened to your face, son?" he asked, wiping away the milk at the side of his mouth.

I rubbed the swollen spot he was staring at. It was there when I'd awoken, yet I couldn't recall getting out of bed during the night and falling. In any case, it didn't matter, because the only thing that was important now was insuring the safety of my father. It was a sad thing to realize that he was losing his good sense. And it would worsen, and quickly. Before the day was over, he would accuse me of ripping the front storm door off its hinges and wonder when I was going to have it repaired.

Afterword: Sadly, both M. and his father perished one year later from a fire that started in the kitchen. The preceding manuscript survived and police returned to the property after learning of its contents.

A CHILD'S ADVOCATE

Before this morning you could not have convinced me that anything I uttered as a child had carried the slightest significance to insure its remembrance, by others or myself. The finely edited discourse of the best television and big-screen dramas and the intricately meaningful dialogues one finds in a great book are seldom within the purview of a growing boy to commence and shape. Even the few solemn moments with my closest friends and the girls whom I was sweet on, even these bring from memory the atmosphere of the event more than the actual lines and phrases I contributed.

But early today, after reading that Brad Scofferlin is to stand trial for attempted murder, one statement from my early adolescence has returned, and it deserves examination because of its possible impact on a person's life.

The chubber Brad accused our eighth-grade English teacher, Mr. Lesniak, of slapping his face, and he stuck with his preposterous story, despite the fact that his seat was at the center in the front row. Twenty–two classmates beside and behind him knew the event had not happened. If there is any fairness due Brad, it may be that he merely perpetuated the lie. His mother, recognized throughout the community as a chronically querulous woman, could have been its inventor. But whatever the lie's provenance, Mrs. Scofferlin got behind the matter and with the steady rumble of a disintegrating wheel bearing, pushed it into the faces of school officials. She was after Mr. Lesniak's dismissal, everyone said. He was unmarried and in only his second year of teaching in our rural district. As a result of her persistence, a stranger was summoned to hear Brad's complaint. I learned this while sitting in Mr. Lesniak's room and waiting for him to end a conversation with another teacher out in the hall and tell me what I was to do.

When he finally entered the room, he was laughing to himself, but he willingly shared the point of it.

"You know Bradley is holding to this thing that I struck him in full view of you and the remainder of the class. Well, Roger, his mother has now wrangled the administration into inviting down a fellow for a visit to this fine institution, and they're calling him the Child Advocate. But I'm thinking they should have employed an apostrophe *s* rather than the double noun. What do you think?"

I shrugged. Whereupon he lowered himself to my level and narrowed his eyes. He was not an overly big man, but he appeared ruggedly fit and always collected.

"What?" I said nervously.

"Roger," he addressed me in a slow, creepy voice, "you're not the Child Advocate, are you?"

It was a joke of some kind, but I didn't get it. At least not right then.

"Forget it!" he said. "What are we going to have you do today? Because you didn't read any of the stories this week, it would be foolish of me to expect you to do it now. You'll just stare at the book. What about the vocabulary? Why didn't you look up the words?"

"It takes too long to find them," I said brashly.

"That's because you *never* look them up. It takes ten seconds to search for a word."

He unstrapped the watch from his wrist and gave it to me. Then he reached for the dictionary on his desk and placed it on mine.

"Open it to any page you want."

I just opened it.

"All right. Give me a word. Then time how long it takes me to locate it."

I just sat there.

"On King!" he shouted, a phrase that had been meaningless until one of my undergraduates, twenty-five years later, turned in a paper on early television programming, and I learned about Sergeant Preston of the Royal Canadian Mounted Police and his dog.

"Stopwatch," I had muttered back then, a telling sign of my

94

lack of creative spontaneity.

Flip, flip, flip. Flip, flip. His index finger stopped here, there. Its movement reminded me of a mouse unaware it was being observed, but the finger was under the word. Time: 8 seconds.

"Easy, huh? Let's have another."

I sat there, dumb.

"You're planning to be late for your funeral, aren't you?"

"Heavy metal," I blurted out.

He harrumphed or something, then flip, flip, the finger probed. There was the entry. Time: 7 seconds.

"To your surprise, I'm sure."

He was right about that. The following day I looked the word up to show to my friends. Jesse Walker had screwed up his face and exclaimed, "Why is that in the dictionary anyway? I hate that kind of music."

"So you want me to look up the words and their definitions, then I can leave?"

"I don't think so," he said. "You'll just mosey through it like a horse my mother once owned who never got to where he wanted. No, you can learn the definitions when you feel like it, even if that's way in the future. For now, I want you just to look up the words. There are twenty of them. If you can find each one under thirty seconds, you can be out of here in what?"

When I didn't answer, he whacked my shoulder with some force. "I asked you a question, Roger."

"What?" I said.

"Twenty words, thirty seconds for each. How long before you can leave?"

I was thinking, I swear.

"Oh *sacre bleu*," he said. "Your math stinks as much as your English."

"Ten minutes," I blurted out, hoping my mental calculator had not made a mistake.

"Well blessed be the Lord and his band of cronies! There's hope for you yet. Now give me back my watch."

I handed the watch over.

"Okay," he said, standing behind me, "now make use of those words at the top of each page. They're called rubrics, and they're the first and last word on the page. And by the way, if you rip a page, you will not get out of here any time soon. Are you ready?"

How could I not be. I had figured to be detained for a minimum of one hour. He continued to stand over me as I searched out each word and slid a confirming finger beneath it. When I dallied, he rapped his knuckles against my shoulder and urged me to "keep moving."

Too many students were in danger of failing their classes for the entire year, but every student knew such a catastrophe would not be allowed, and sure enough, the school folk devised their plan to account for our future passing. It was called Academic Intervention, or AI as the teachers usually referred to it, which brought a titter from most of us.

"I'm impressed," said Mr. Lesniak. "I would have bet part of a paycheck that none of you ever heard of Artificial Intelligence."

This brought more tittering because in our farming community AI had nothing to do with intelligence; it had only to do with the black rubber glove that extended to one's elbow, the entire length of which was then inserted into the back end of a cow.

The first step of the school's AI brought parents into the building following dismissal and had them sit down with the teachers of their failing offspring, the principal, and the guidance counselor, everybody together in one office. Students in trouble were rarely asked to be at the convocation.

Lesniak hated the plan, and he told our class so.

"There's a word that has become popular. That word is *empowerment*. Somebody above us teachers, who supposedly has power, is giving it to us. We in turn will give it to all of you."

"What kind of power do you have, Mr. Lesniak?" Tricia Benton asked. She was a serious student who was not afraid to ask anything of our teachers, and although it had always seemed to me that a peppering of ridicule accompanied each of her questions, not a teacher seemed to mind. They always answered her forthrightly.

"Hmmm, I don't know that I have any power, Tricia. In fact, judging from what I've been seeing everywhere around me, I'm inclined to think there has been an abdication of power and that a trick is being played on all of us."

I liked Mr. Lesniak. He was fair, often comical, downright wacky at times, and I think he liked us kids. Yet there were times when I could not follow what he was saying because he would mix big words with small. So he lost me as he talked about Academic Intervention, abdication of power, and the playing of a trick. But the following day provided me with an opportunity to better understand the matter.

It was the seventh period and I was in study hall. The Ignuts behind me was flicking tiny wads of paper at the back of my head. After about the thirtieth time, I turned around and lunged at him, forcing him from his desk and onto the floor. To the day's substitute, it was of no significance that this fellow was lying amidst his own array of wadded paper. Like the basketball player who throws the second punch, I was declared the one for punishment and sent to the principal's office.

Mr. Lesniak was there, appearing as if he was about to take his exit, and the principal, X. Jerome White, told me to come right in.

"What have you done, Roger?" Mr. Lesniak asked.

"He was fighting," said X. Jerome.

"I didn't even throw a punch," I said.

"You did attack another student. I don't think Mrs. Balfour has any reason to lie."

"Well, I was getting my head blitzed with paper wads and she didn't even notice!"

"Yes, when she called, she mentioned the paper. It's all over the floor. And because Mrs. Balfour acted quickly enough so that no one was hurt, I am going to let you off easy. You're to return to her study hall and pick up that paper that's on the floor."

"No I'm not!" I said. "It's not my paper."

"Roger, don't try my patience! I'm letting you off easy."

97

"It isn't my paper," I said. "Why don't *you* go pick it up?"

Mr. Lesniak jumped in to rescue me from my mouth. "Let's go, Roger."

"I'm not doing it."

"Yes, you are," he said. "And I'm going to help."

We walked the length of the school to the study hall. Mr. Lesniak briefly looked through the window of the door, and then with a slight tap on the glass, we entered the room with him in the lead.

"Just ignore us," he said to Mrs. Balfour who looked up from a paperback with a mammoth on its cover. Without any signal to me, he immediately went among the rows and started picking up the paper strewn all over, paying little attention to the students, although he did speak a friendly word at floor level to a couple. Several seconds elapsed before I joined him in the action, beginning at the other side of the room.

When we finished, we left as unobtrusively as we had entered, this time myself leading the way.

Outside in the hall he said: "I think you're supposed to stay, Roger."

"I know that. Only I want to say again it wasn't my paper. I didn't throw—"

He interrupted. "Roger! It was paper. What did it take us? Forty-five seconds, maybe, to pick the stuff up off the floor?"

"But you don't believe me. You think all of that was my paper. Or at least some of it, and it wasn't. It was all Wilson's."

"No, I don't. What makes you say that?"

"You didn't say anything to him."

"Until you mentioned his name just this moment I had no idea whose paper it was."

"But he did to you what he did to me," I said.

"He shot a paper wad at me?"

"He missed. It's still on the floor."

He turned around and took the few steps that put him back at the door to the study hall. He peered through the window.

"I see it," he muttered in a devilish tone, and he re-entered the room and retrieved the piece of paper, giving but a glance at Wilson who watched from behind a grin that was eating and enjoying a little shit.

When he returned to the hall, he said, "You better go on in now."

"Aren't you going to do anything to him?"

"I just did."

He could see that his answer hadn't satisfied me. He checked his watch.

"The day's almost over. All right, let's take a walk."

We hadn't gone three paces when he began his explanation, mindless of other students who passed us in the hall.

"When I was your age, Roger, if a student like Wilson had done what he just did to me, the teacher would have had him out of his seat, off the floor, and against the wall."

That was all he was able to get out as a raucous fight erupted at the other end of the hall, and I could see arms flailing and lot of pushing and shoving, along with an instant gathering of many yelling onlookers. Mr. Lesniak leaped into action and raced to the fight. I was intending to follow until dapper Mr. Garfield, stepping out of his room, pointed a finger on my behalf in the other direction.

I had Mr. Lesniak the third period, and the next day, while class was underway, the Superintendent of our school district, with X. Jerome White trailing behind, opened the door without knocking and sauntered in. Mr. Lesniak formed an expression that might have been reserved for Ed McMahon delivering a check the size of a pool table, and for a moment he started to say something that sounded to me like we were on the same nasty thinking wavelength, but then he reversed himself and simply said, "Yes?"

X. Jerome did the talking while the Super ran a grave eye, like a searchlight, over the class. "Five minutes before the period ends, send six or seven of your students to my office."

"Any six or seven in particular?" Mr. Lesniak asked

sportively.

Apparently this question was out-of-line because the Super instantly detached his attention from the rest of us and pinned it on Mr. Lesniak. The man's face was an enormous unfriendly stone.

At that moment none of us was aware that we were to be questioned concerning Brad Scofferlin's accusation of Mr. Lesniak. But no sooner had we filed into the principal's office than X. Jerome introduced the man who had been summoned from elsewhere to look into the matter.

"He's what is called a Child Advocate," explained X. Jerome to us kids. "You can tell him anything. It will not get any of you into trouble. Do you understand?"

Addressing the man himself whom I remember as being dressed rather shabbily and wearing shoes that were muddied around the heels, I asked, "Is that really what you're called?"

Assuming that I needed further assurance and desperately wanting to comply, he angled to a slight crouch to reduce the height between us and relaxed the lines in his face. "Yes, that's my title. I'm this region's Child Advocate. And like your principal just told you, you can tell me anything. I'm on your side. That's what Child Advocate means. I'm on your side."

I got it, I remember thinking, Mr. Lesniak's morsel about the omitted apostrophe *s* (I wasn't completely lost when it came to punctuation; it just took me a while), and it must have showed, for the Super said, "Is there something funny, son?"

You bet there was, I wanted to say, but he really didn't look the type who believed anything concerning education should ever be humorous. So I didn't answer, and both the advocate and X. Jerome began to interrogate us about what took place during the period when Mr. Lesniak was supposed to have struck Brad. Then, afterwards, the advocate met with each of us individually and asked a few more questions.

There wasn't any need for the one-on-one sessions. Jesse Walker, right at the start, probably had spoken for everyone when he told the three adults in the room that "The chubber is just looking for attention." Then with his mouth Jesse made a noise faintly resembling released gas to add a final emphasis to his judgment of classmate Brad Scofferlin.

The following day all us kids who had undergone questioning got word that Brad's mother was spreading the lie that we had been handpicked by Mr. Lesniak because we said what he had wanted us to say. That we were his personal favorites, unlike her son Bradley. Hearing this, Jesse and I both suggested we find Brad and slap him silly, no matter that it was his mother, not him, who was painting us as brown-nosers. It turned out there wasn't a need.

Mrs. Scofferlin marched into Mr. Lesniak's room after the end of the school day while I was working the bejeezus out of pronouns. My friend Jesse was on hand as well, waiting for my release.

"You're not going to get away with this," she threatened Mr. Lesniak, who was seated behind his desk. She looked mean and especially vindictive, and I can remember wondering if she was going to reach out and physically strike him. "You can get your precious little pets to say to the administration anything you want, but it isn't going to work!"

"Now you hold on one minute."

"You don't order me to do anything!"

"Hold your tongue, lady," said Mr. Lesniak, rising ominously. "There's something important you need to hear. Your boy Bradley?"

"What about Bradley?"

"I don't like him. Not one iota."

"How dare you!"

"Oh, I'm perfectly serious. I cannot stand your son. He's lazy and, in my opinion, spoiled beyond repair."

Mrs. Scofferlin glanced over at Jesse and me, disbelief displayed on her face amidst the nutty anger. Disbelief not because Mr. Lesniak didn't like her son—she must have already been thinking that—but because he was stating his feelings before two eighth-graders. Jesse, I could see, was himself somewhat

101

disbelieving for the same reason, but I was not. I had been in Mr. Lesniak's presence enough in recent weeks to realize he was not afraid to say what was on his mind to a thirteen year-old. When he talked in similar fashion to me, I had the feeling that he was waiting for the day when I would speak up and continue the conversation once he finished with everything he had to say.

In the moment of silence that followed, Mr. Lesniak strode around to the front of his desk while Mrs. Scofferlin appeared to be regrouping. Her facial expression now displayed signs of cunning.

"You might see yourself as funny and cute," she finally said to Mr. Lesniak, "but when I report to the administration and the school board what you just said to me in front of these boys, I don't believe they will think any of it is funny."

"Don't leave just yet," Mr. Lesniak responded tonelessly, taking still another step at her. "I've more you need to hear. I want to make certain you understand the logic of this matter. Not only do I not like your son much—or you, for that matter, Mrs. Scofferlin—but if Bradley is to pass my course and move on, he will have to do it on his own. I will teach him according to what is expected of me in my contract with this school district, but if he wants help, he will need to ask for it. He will need to ask ME for it. You see, I don't give a hoot if your son passes or fails. He can head straight down the proverbial tubes. Which brings up the illogic of your accusation against me. I wouldn't expend the slightest energy to slap the face of anyone I dislike. And that includes you and your son."

With his final words on the subject to Lydia Scofferlin, the thought had occurred to me that Mr. Lesniak *might* finally have stepped over the line. Fuming, but in no way defeated, she spun around, left the room, and he returned to sitting behind his desk. Only once did he glance at Jesse and myself. I completed the exercises on the pronouns, and together we headed out. Once in the hallway Jesse turned back.

"Hey, Mr. Lesniak! I've a question. Would you ever slap Roger and me?"

Mr. Lesniak barely shook his head. "No," he said quietly.

I understood then where Jesse was coming from, as a cloud of disappointment settled on my friend.

"With you fellows, I would probably kick your tails to kingdom come."

*

In the months to follow it seemed there was very little of the Scofferlin thing mentioned anywhere, and in the end it appeared to have simply disappeared through confrontation's own principles for attrition. There was no AI for Brad (I presumed Mr. Lesniak successfully had held his ground and wouldn't agree to it unless asked by Brad or his mother, and of course that must have been out of the question), and so he failed English, meaning he had to attend summer school in order to be a freshman. Summer school was a less stringent form of Academic Intervention and suited students like Brad Scofferlin who never did much of anything. Summer school, depending on the teacher, sometimes required that students like Brad simply do several weeks more of nothing, and then, and only then, could they move on to the next grade and continue with their ever-growing torpidity. No one had ever inquired of us kids what we thought of AI but, in the case of the lying chubber, Jesse said if the question arose his recommendation would include use of the glove.

As for Mr. Lesniak, obviously he had not been fired, because he returned to teach the next semester.

That summer following the Scofferlin affair I started lifting weights with my father. I liked football and the school sponsored a j.v. squad. My father was for it because he saw that I had athletic ability, plus he entertained the hope that playing sports would somehow spur some academic interests, a position my mother prematurely doubted but went along with so that her boy Roger would be happy.

My father, young farmer though he was and in great shape because of the hard, physical labor, nonetheless continued to weightlift, an activity initiated in his teenage years, and I duplicated what he did each evening, only with fewer reps and using less weight. We worked out in an old lighted, board-and batten shed behind the house, careful not to drop any bars on Muffin and her kittens who ran about helter-skelter from one minute to the next. With their arrival Mom had ordered they stay outside the house where accidents wouldn't be a problem. They were a riot to watch and my father and I broke out laughing more than once while in the middle of a jerk. At first Muffin's role was one of just being there for her offspring, but in time they became frisky, and eventually, having added some size and weight to themselves, they started to test their mother, as well as Shank, our long-haired male. Once that happened, either Muffin or Shank would haul off and give the upstart a what-for, at times clamping the offender good and tight between their jaws. I worried for the young ones and would run off the older pair when this happened. My father, however, pointed out that the small ones were never really injured, and I took the time to examine a couple to learn the truth of that for myself.

By summer's end, any chance that I myself might be labeled a chubber was buried in muscle that was rapidly firming up. I made the j.v. squad with no regrets.

At school I completed the assigned work and did my best to keep up my grades to avoid becoming ineligible academically and being dropped from the team. Although I had a different teacher this year for English, Mr. Lesniak was the supervisor for one of my study halls, and he did not assign seats, except that whatever seat you plopped into on day one, that was your seat for the remainder of the term. I grabbed the first desk in the first row, right next to the door.

Near the start of the Thanksgiving break, with the door to the room open, I couldn't help but listen to a conversation out in the hall.

"Your problem is, you treat your students like children. That's what created your trouble with the Scofferlin boy. I'd recommend you treat them as the young adults they are." This was Mr.

Garfield, my world geography teacher, lecturing Mr. Lesniak.

"You mean I should have them call me by my first name, as you do?"

"It would be a start. It lets them know you're a friend and that you consider them the same. That you're not *just* their teacher."

Ted Garfield, who was probably only a few years older than Mr. Lesniak insisted that his students call him "Ted," but my parents insisted otherwise. They taught me to address my teachers by Mr, Miss, or Mrs. I never told this to Mr. Garfield and he continued urging me to call him by his first name, but I never once did.

Mr. Garfield struck me as a person too sure of himself and his opinions, and he must have impressed Mr. Lesniak in the same way.

"Have you really thought this out, Ted?" By now I believed I knew Mr. Lesniak fairly well and that the new tone to his words was somewhat mocking. Even addressing Mr. Garfield by his first name, this too made me suspicious.

"Of course I've thought about it. And I've read more than a few books on the subject. Have you ever stepped away long enough from reading your all-precious fiction that you can say the same?"

Mr. Lesniak stuck his head inside the room to see if any problems were developing. He winked at me and mouthed the words, "Are you enjoying this, Roger?"

Something then occurred to me that, when it had happened, did not meant very much. Last year, in advance of a test, Tricia Benton had asked Mr. Lesniak what we had to know to prepare, and he replied with "Everything between page this and page that, plus everything we talked about."

"But everything won't be on the test," Tricia objected. "Why not tell us exactly what's on it so we can study for just those things and not waste time on the others?"

"If I ever do that, you kids remember to be insulted. Because what I'll be saying is that I think you're too stupid and irresponsible to handle anything more than what is actually on the test."

Mr. Garfield wrote outlines on the board, then handed out sheets of the exact same thing. What was on the sheets was on the tests, nothing more, nothing less. Other material that we had read in the textbook or discussed in class never appeared. Mr. Garfield told his classes exactly what would be included in their tests.

Sitting in my study hall seat near the door that day and listening to my teachers talk, I learned Mr. Lesniak did not care very much for his colleague.

And something else I learned at that same moment is to think about the things I do and, more, think about those things that are done to me. It was my first interest in psychology, one might say, as I began to realize that what things look like and what they sound like coming from others isn't necessarily what they are.

I have never forgotten Mr. Lesniak's final words to Mr. Garfield that day:

"Send your uncle to the store for cigarettes at three in the morning and you probably won't worry about him, Ted. Send a ten-year old, I would hope you do. Regarding kids as adults is little more than a means to absolve yourself of the guilt so you need not worry very much about them."

*

January arrived and with it the second semester of my freshman year. My schedule changed hardly at all. I had the same study hall with Mr. Lesniak, except several upperclassmen were added to it, among them Wilson who, it became clear, had not forgotten that he flicked a paper wad at Mr. Lesniak and that it was the teacher who retrieved it off the floor and discarded it into the waste basket. Wilson was taller now than when I had trouble with him, but my training with the weights kept us on equal footing, maybe even gave me the edge. Whatever the reason, Wilson ignored me from the start and concentrated on Mr. Lesniak.

His actions, intended to disrupt the study hall and show up Mr. Lesniak, are too numerous to mention here. They inspired me to doubt Mr. Lesniak whom I had come to think of as something close to a friend, but I did not doubt him for long.

One afternoon around midterm, Mr. Lesniak, without provocation, got up from his desk and walked to within a few feet of Wilson sitting near the back of row five. Between his fingers was a paper wad. He flicked it. It missed Wilson by a few inches and landed on the floor.

"Man," said Wilson, recoiling with ridicule, "don't go hurling none o' your boogers in my direction."

His fellow upperclassmen laughed and set their eyes on Mr. Lesniak.

"It was a paper wad," Mr. Lesniak said, and he uttered the words inside a tone implying great amicability.

"Yeah, well, maybe," said Wilson, but he stopped himself from saying anything further, and the look on his face was the same look that was on every student's face, mine included. And that look said that something strange was underway.

"Pick it up," Mr. Lesniak said to Wilson.

"Hey, it isn't mine. I didn't throw it there."

"Excuse me," said Mr. Lesniak with an even bigger smile than the one before. "Would you please pick it up? I would much appreciate it if you did."

Wilson met Mr. Lesniak's eyes, kept them there for a time, then leaned over and snatched the paper wad off the floor, all the while making a scene of it. When he was straight up again and Mr. Lesniak's hand was outstretched to accept the prize, he said, "Naw, can't do it. It isn't mine," and he let the tiny piece of paper fall to the floor once more.

The study hall was now as silent as it would ever be.

Mr. Lesniak ran a hand over his forehead.

"Son—

"I'm not your son!"

"Mr. Wilson, I'm getting the idea that you're a person who does whatever he wants to do."

"I won't let myself get pushed around," answered Wilson. "By anyone."

Mr. Lesniak slowly nodded in a display of understanding.

"If that piece of paper belonged to me, I would pick it up," Wilson added. "But it doesn't."

"I see," said Mr. Lesniak. "So had I asked you to pick up the paper wad from a year ago—I'm sure you know what I'm referring to—you would have?"

Wilson moved his head without meaning and offered no reply.

"At least there lives a grain of honesty in you," Mr. Lesniak said. "Sadly, though, it's not enough." He swung away from Wilson and looked at us others. "Now the rest of you people, I want you to get out of here," he said.

No one moved, simply because we didn't understand what was happening. Mr. Lesniak left Wilson's aisle and stepped over to the door.

"Everyone! Get out! Go to the library, the gym, or just roam the hall and dodge the monitors. Everyone but Wilson and Roger."

Rest assured I was surprised, to say the least!

"Let's go. Move."

Boys and girls, a few seniors and several juniors, the remainder my freshmen classmates, dubiously rose from their desks and shuffled up the aisles and out of the room. When they were gone, Mr. Lesniak took his keys from a pocket, then reached around to the outside of the door and locked it.

"Why'd you want him to stay?" Wilson asked, meaning me. His voice was full of uncertainty.

Mr. Lesniak shook a finger at him as if to say, "I'm glad you reminded me," and went to the rear of the room where there was a closet. He opened it and pulled out a giant sheet of poster board with pictures of Ernest Hemingway, John Steinbeck, Carson McCullers, Willa Cather, and several other American authors attached.

"Roger! Take this board and hold it over the window on the door so that no one can see inside."

Yes, I've written the words here as if I had understood them the instant they were said. Truth is, I was so dumbfounded by what was happening that Mr. Lesniak had to say them again, the second time adopting the kind of patience you might expect to be allotted a three-year old. But finally I accepted the large poster board and pressed it to the inside of the window on the door, the photos of the authors staring back at me and over my shoulders to the unfolding scene.

"Now let's get started," Mr. Lesniak announced to Wilson, and as I glanced backward, he rubbed his hands together with nothing less than anticipation. "Here's how it's going to work. You, son, are going to bend over and pick up that paper wad from the floor. And I promise to wipe your little smartass across every inch of the floor and the walls until you do. Once that's done, you'll make your own promise to never again show me disrespect. Any questions?"

Wilson hadn't yet bought into things.

"Go on. Say what you're thinking," Mr. Lesniak urged him.

"You're going to lose your job over this," said Wilson.

"And you think this job of working with the likes of you is something to be treasured and protected?"

With that I turned completely around so I could see both Mr. Lesniak and Wilson. I held the poster to the window with my back.

Wilson appeared to be wrestling inside with another concern.

"Once you leave this room again," said Mr. Lesniak, "you can tell the others whatever you want. Make up a fantastic tale and lie to them, I don't care. Roger doesn't either. He won't contradict your story, will you, Roger?"

I shook my head, not entirely sure to what I was agreeing. But soon enough I did, and I understood too what Mr. Lesniak was already in possession of: no one would believe Wilson if he lied. Not because he was such a poor liar, but because they had come into some strange new knowledge about Mr. Lesniak.

Wilson, seated at his desk, continued to have trouble making up his mind, and Mr. Lesniak approached him on the far side of the room. This meant that Wilson, if he decided to up and run, might have a chance to make the door without Mr. Lesniak catching him.

In a way it was a dare and I thought Wilson saw it the same.

The look that had formed on Mr. Lesniak's face was far different. It told me, young eighth-grader though I was and, doubtlessly, bug-eyed at the time, that Mr. Lesniak not only was going to wipe the floor with Wilson and care not a whit if he lost his job as a result, but also that he was doing this troublemaker the biggest favor he would ever have done for him in his early years.

"Well, what's it going to be?"

I was making the bet inside my head, and Wilson soon paid off. He bent over and captured the paper wad.

"Thank you," said Mr. Lesniak. "Now you can go and join the others, wherever they may be. And don't forget the part about respect."

Wilson then rose from his seat and made for the door. I took away the poster, but let him get himself out.

The bell rang signaling an end to the study hall.

"Just leave the poster on a desk," Mr. Lesniak said to me. Then, something resembling a smile replaced the earlier look, and as I myself was about to exit the room, he asked, "Roger, do you think it's too late to give a good slap to our boy Bradley? I mean a real slap?"

*

Not long after this incident with Wilson, Mr. Lesniak would receive his tenure, but when another September arrived, he was nowhere to be found. Some people in town then circulated the story the school board only granted him tenure in exchange for his agreement to resign. They'd wanted to fire him, but he'd threatened a lawsuit. Others, like Jesse and myself, hadn't believed that he would ever make a deal of any kind and that he left because ours was a district for which he simply no longer wanted to work.

Jesse and I missed him during our remaining years. Wilson told me he did, too. Brad and Lydia, I know firsthand, were gleeful following his departure. And it was then I realized why I had answered Mr. Lesniak's question in the way I did. But it is only today that I realize the significance of my words.

From grade one I never liked Brad Scofferlin. Back then I would have called it hate.

"Leave him alone," I had said to Mr. Lesniak.

"Really, Roger?"

"Yes. Just leave him be. Let him become whatever he becomes."

SUFFIX AND BOLD

Before a tense bladder orders him to the bathroom, he keyboards this on the computer:

At 60, it seemed to Faldowski the principal objective of his entire adult life had been to keep the gun away from his head.

When he re-emerges, knowing he failed once again to relax his muscles, the screensaver of cosmic close-ups of Jupiter, Andromeda, and other points eternal has not appeared. Yet Hester has. Hip cocked, drink in hand, a puddle of amusement flooding her pampered face, his wife of thirty-two years is reading his autobiographical revelation.

When finished, she levels a finger at the lone sentence. "Well, let's have it," she says and wags the probe with a sharp painted nail as though the monitor has asked her to relieve a troublesome itch. "Success or failure? Either way, you must have explored that cavern of deplorable enamel with the revolver on at least one occasion. My guess? You discovered you couldn't trust yourself."

Faldowski's face, the size of an undersized door that's been kicked in habitually despite the protection of numerous locks, collapses out of the disappearing hope she will ever see his frustration.

"Answer me this. When you slipped the barrel between your lips, did you...?"

He watches as her tongue performs a serpentine medley of actions. Such behavior would be obscene in another five years; it was already getting close. "I pressed it against my temple," he tells her. "I never placed it in my mouth."

"Oh really? What about bullets? Did you load the gun? Or did you put up an empty pistol and...?"

" ... And what, Hester?"

Her upper body joins in the fun with a shrinking concentricity of bobs, like the bounce of an underinflated ball.

"Did you—you know—shake?" The vertical motion changes to a vibratory one as she herself shakes, all over, along with her earrings, large slender hoops alive with glitter that would fare better on an African woman than they do on this pale translucent flesh stretched over a deceptively strong trellis. When he's in the flower garden and comes across the gauzy home of some destructive insect, Faldowski is reminded of his wife, and a fiery thought released on the big screen at the front of his brain produces a smile. "Did your finger on the trigger tremble while you sobbed *boohoo, boohoo?* What I'm asking, my dear Faldowski, is this: Were you the proverbial wreck of a man?"

"I hate you, Hester. More than anything in the world, I hate you. You're the reason—"

"—Oh, read your goddamn words, love," she interrupts while forcing herself to swallow. She has no patience for a husband's emotional fabrication. "Long before we ever met, you were an adult. Whatever satisfaction it is that you're seeking, go find it elsewhere."

*

"Where *does* that man get his satisfaction?" is sometimes the topic of conversation by the residents of the fertilized and manicured neighborhood, if they aren't overworking their jobs and the Internet, children and Jesus; if they're able to hone their thinking, which grows more muddled and infantile everyday because of contemporary disingenuous life, so apparent it's, paradoxically, become invisible in their churches, schools, and government. Mostly, the residents observe their much older neighbor. For example, they've noted that Faldowski has never been unfriendly at the annual block parties. And yet it seems he doesn't have any friends. They certainly do not admit of themselves as such, and Ram Corbin, who lives in the corner house framed by large azaleas and the biggest lawn, can be counted on to remind them of one reason for this by clowning a hillbilly's face that suggests misaligned, rotten teeth. The wives offer a polite laugh to this stunt, which is more grotesque than accurate, but still they shudder.

Sometimes the group watches Hester who they've noted is likewise without friends. A few of the women have approached her. But what is just as clear to them is she doesn't want any friends. While critical of this behavior, they also, oddly, admire it, evident in their tone, subtle warnings to each other regarding the future. This deliberate avoidance of affability is behind the sole vote they give to Hester. All others go to Faldowski.

And as anyone would expect, there are times when Faldowski and Hester together as man and wife grab everyone's focus. The observation on these occasions is that neither spouse acts as a confidant to the other; and without children, they ask, isn't that odd?

*

When she walks off after noticing that her glass is empty, Faldowski steps over to the mouse and keyboard. He hasn't saved what's on the screen (he's no idea why he typed it) and he has no thoughts that logically follow the statement. Just for a moment he jiggles the mouse and as if by design, it lowers a menu with the cursor on "Clear." The message does not elude him and he smiles to himself. The edginess somewhat removed, he closes the window, casting his words into the black hole of cyberspace reserved for trash. However, he will not forget what he wrote, and in the days ahead he will type out another statement that is quite similar in appearance, but significantly different in meaning.

In the evening he and Hester do what they've done for quite some time: they have dinner together. In fact, they prepare the meal, Hester in charge of the main course and dessert, while Faldowski tosses the salad, which includes radishes, scores of cauliflower and broccoli florets, carrot coins, water chestnuts, sprouts. For him, these items are what make a salad, and so he leaves much of the leaf behind on the chopping block. It is just the opposite with Hester, which explains Faldowski's involvement.

They talk while they eat, they always have. Their table is not the extended kind imagined by others, the kind that fits with a spacious home and seemingly stretches to infinity; their table is small, square. And where do they sit? Not across from each other, as their earlier discourse might suggest, as the neighbors would conclude. No, Faldowski and Hester sit adjacent to each other where one has on occasion nudged the other after a good line, sometimes funny, sometimes not. Once, Hester's agreeable retort to a joke about the President was so hilariously insightful that Faldowski nudged her featherweight body right off the chair onto the parquet floor. He suggested she should remain there as a rug. She replied that he was the one accustomed to getting trampled. Tonight, Hester throws out a question neither has asked in at least a decade.

"Why do you think we've not divorced?"

They are in only the first course of the meal, and Faldowski is annoyed with the tongs, a new pair purchased just yesterday at the local Williams-Sonoma, because while they are great for picking up the Romaine, they are useless for snatching from the wide circular bowl the small pieces of his favorite vegetables. He gives up and reaches in with his hand, Ethiopian-style, to fish out a collection of small prizes.

"In this state," he says, crunching raw cauliflower, "you can divorce me, and I can divorce you. *We* don't have to agree."

"Answer, Br'er Rabbit."

"You've not divorced your Faldowski, and never will. And that, Hester, is because you are inherently lazy."

"Really!" she says, genuinely surprised at what he's come up with. She thinks for a minute and more, time enough for him to eat much of the cauliflower and part of the broccoli. Finally she offers this: "Might it not be something else entirely? Like, how easy it is to shape and manage you, my very own Mr. Putty Boy. And because of that, I am not unhappy. It is a thing I require, and you guarantee its fulfillment. Isn't it possible that's the reason I've not

116

filed in all these years?"

Faldowski considers her explanation, throughout chomping and chewing, then nods in the patently familiar manner that says, *"Maybe, maybe not."*

"Now, what about you?"

"Yes, what about me? Why haven't I rid my life of you? Any man in his right mind certainly would have, don't you think?"

Faldowski has addressed the question to himself many times, and sometimes it seems the reason is the same he's just accused Hester of. Yet he has no history of indolence; he's always been a moderately hard worker. Still, there was one job that defeated him, when every thing he did, every move he made, was thrown back in his face, so that eventually he slacked off and let the whole thing go on as it had. Isn't that what has unfolded in this marriage? Is he too fatigued, altogether too beaten down to seek a divorce? He's aware the common belief in the neighborhood is that Hester's the bitch and he's the victim. And Hester, too, is aware of this viewpoint, as she mockingly told him he could make something positive out of the matter if he *"hung"* with the husbands. She'd watched a certain Oprah show and convinced herself that every man desired to be on the *down low*, in spite of Faldowski telling her he couldn't stand to look at another man's naked buttocks, much less the front appendage, and that his revulsion went all the way back to junior high school.

"Hello in there?"

"I don't have an answer," he says. "Not yet."

*

It is impossible for the neighbors to make anything out of Faldowski and Hester's relationship. Although they believe they can understand how it came about, they're unable to reconcile its long continuation with their own recent divorces. For a while there was talk one or the other had the money, and a divorce would mean one or the other would no longer have it. Then Ram Corbin's wife, Skeeter, a teacher's aide at the high school, learned from its oldest teacher, who had known the parents of both Faldowski and Hester, that each received an inheritance.

After that, the search for the truth turned vulgar. Fatty Benton from the end of the street offered that Hester wasn't leaving because "Faldowski must be a horse beneath the covers," *ha-ha*. This was cancelled quickly by another neighbor who imitated Ram Corbin's hillbilly, which dared Ram Corbin to say, "Maybe she's like my sweetie and that part doesn't matter as much." And while Skeeter laughed because fellating her husband is, indeed, her favorite sex, Marc Waverly, a trivia buff on all things Mafia, said, "A man who doesn't make time for his teeth can never be a real man."

*

It is Saturday, this year's Block Party Day for the neighborhood. Hester and Faldowski are reminded of the annual event when they peer out their windows in the morning and see their many neighbors setting up tables, some in backyards, others who aren't barbecuing, out front. Hester looks in the refrigerator, tells Faldowski they need to go to the store. At the corner, a similar scenario is underway at the Corbins, who haven't overlooked the party, but have forgotten to get the necessary groceries earlier in the week, especially the hot sausage, Ram's specialty that he does on the grill with loads of onion. Waiting on his wife, he stares out a window.

As the garage door elevates on the west side of the street, sunshine dashes in to spotlight the burgundy Buick, always immaculately clean and shined. Ram grins to himself; he's watched this episode before.

"Skeeter!" he calls.

"Right there!"

Seconds later, Hester and Faldowski are visible descending the few steps outside the door leading from the kitchen to the rear of the garage, and he attempts to get behind the wheel. Hester shoos him like a chicken to the vehicle's passenger side.

"Ah, you missed it, Skeeter! You missed it!"

"Just about there!"

Already at the supermarket when the Corbins arrive are Fatty Benton, who's filling a cart with beer and soda, and Marc Waverly who is sharing his cart with the wife of another neighbor. They've all driven at speeds faster than Hester.

It's Fatty Benton who first sees the older couple as they enter the store and he alerts the others. The group becomes immobile, each person straining not to make a face, but not entirely succeeding.

Faldowski reaches for a cart and shakes it violently loose from the one with which it is copulating, but it's Hester who takes immediate control. Then down the aisle nearest, stacked with sandwich and salad dressings. With Faldowski at her side, Hester directs: *Get this. Get that. Two of those. That's less per ounce than the bigger size, don't argue.* Then comes a moment when Hester strays from the cart in order to read a label, and in a flash Faldowski moves in and wraps his hands around the plastic handle. He's ready to roll. When Hester turns back, Faldowski holds up a palm and says, "I've got the conn."

The surveillance team, hovering in front of the pickles and relish, looks at one another.

"Did he say what I...?"

"'I've got the con.'"

There's unexpected illumination, strange illumination, they think, of this odd couple, but they accept it. God knows they've needed some inroad into who the hell Faldowski and Hester are.

Fatty Benton asks his question even as he doubts it and wonders if he is being politically incorrect: "Could they be gypsies?"

"No way," says Ram Corbin, who realizes the effectiveness of his hillbilly impersonation is probably over, as the couple is showing some sophistication.

Trying to recollect, Skeeter Corbin says, "That group in North Carolina. There's a entire town of them."

"The Travelers or something," Waverly says. And with this each of them remembers the story on *60 Minutes* about a clannish people who devote themselves to theft and the defrauding of others outside their group, including the very old.

The woman with Waverly is attempting to say something, and they finally let her. She jabs an almost secret finger toward the front of the store and mentions the sheet of paper attached to the side of each cash register. It's a warning to till-tappers they'll be prosecuted to the fullest extent of the law. Fatty Benton wants to know how the scam works, but Ram Corbin says "Later" because Hester and Faldowski have reversed direction and are now moving toward the group.

Hester stops in the middle of them and, in place of a smile, crimps her lips as though they were formed of sheet metal. She reaches between Waverly and Skeeter Corbin for a jar of pickles. Faldowski offers his neighbors a real smile; at least it looks real, but who among them can say for certain.

"That was some nifty move you made with your cart," Ram Corbin says while nodding up the aisle. "I brought home a brand new Cub Cadet the other day. It's supposed to spin on a dime. You'll have to come show me how it's done."

Faldowski merely smiles again. He knows more about these people than they think he knows. And he knows about his teeth.

*

The block party, starting around noon, reveals a number of the residents collecting on the big corner lot of the Corbins. They glance time and again at the house of Faldowski and Hester. That's because this year there's a subject of real interest: the old couple as till-tappers, scam artists, thieves. Ram Corbin and Fatty Benton, although neither thinks the other really believes in the possibility, are nonetheless having fun with it, confident in their assumption that no one will tattle to either Faldowski or Hester.

Because Ram asked a cashier at the market for an explanation of the scam after the warning sheet had been posted months ago, he now plays the hypothesizer. He explains to the audience of husbands and wives and a few neighborhood kids how Faldowski's role is likely the diversion.

"What's he do? Smile?" crows a teenage towhead who follows with his own hillbilly imitation. And while Ram points a finger at the boy as though to say "Exactly," he can't help thinking that Waverly's son with his jeans about to fall off his ass would make a good diversion itself.

"So she's the one who actually does the pilfering," says a man wearing a red Henley and standing behind the boy. "She reaches into the till and removes the money?"

"Look closely at the old woman's hands," Fatty Benton says. "They were made for it."

Ram Corbin reclaims the group's attention. "It's worth noting that some who do this are so clever they leave the bills on top the stack and remove only the ones beneath. That way, once the theft is over, the drawer looks untouched. Not until the cashier closes out and does her tally will the store discover it's been robbed."

Up the street Faldowski is tinkering with the table on his front lawn. Hester, after setting out the crepes and other items, went back inside the house where she typically spends the afternoon with her drink. Once the plates and bowls are arranged to his liking, Faldowski flops into one of a half-dozen lawn chairs. Throughout the rest of the year, the weedless grass in the neighborhood receives little foot action, but on Block Party Day the people move directly across it from one house to the next. This year Faldowski takes note his lawn has become the exception. This year families left and right are drifting to the sidewalk. Some continue their safe walk an extra lot down and then double back to his next-door neighbor. Most remember at least to wave to him. Only a handful ventures onto his property to enjoy a crepe, a beer, and exchange some meaninglesss words.

*

Lately, Faldowski has been rolling over in his mind what

Hester said, about his being an adult before they met. And rolling it in the slow manner he does, the answer to her question starts to surface. He thinks he has not divorced her because she has restrained him in her abrasive, empathy-free fashion from acting on his absolutes and generalizations, both habitual. She has done this by merely pointing out the truth. Of course he had contemplated ending his life before they became interested in one another. Like it was yesterday, he remembers the reaction of his older brother when Faldowski told him he was going to kill himself. *"Why the fuck don't you?"* And it wasn't any different, not really, when he'd tried to talk about his depression to his father. One swipe of the big welder's forearm had rearranged Faldowski's teeth for life. There was no one—aunts, uncles, cousins, teachers, friends, and later fellow workers from those early years—who wanted anything to do with him. And the times they did have anything to do with him, always it was to deride Faldowski in order to get a laugh from others. Yes, after crying and feeling humiliated, he'd wanted to kill himself almost every week. So he couldn't blame Hester.

But he couldn't absolve her either. Why was he the one with the eggshell bladder? Why was he always needing to urinate because he could never fully relax himself, when she was the one endlessly navigating the house with a drink in hand? Why was that?

*

It's another Saturday morning and Skeeter Corbin's anxiety throughout the night wants to turn to panic. Husband Ram has not returned home from the office the previous evening. And, sure, there have been occasions when he stayed out very late with friends, but he always was in bed with her before the sun rose. She looks out the window for the hundredth time and sees the police cruiser turn into the driveway of Faldowski and Hester. Her thought is, *Something's happened, and they're at the wrong address.* She watches the two policemen ring the front door bell,

122

but they enter the house before it is answered.

She leaves her own and crosses the street, running. She doesn't bother with the bell, instead shouting "HELLO!" One of the cops steps out from another room.

"Who are you?"

"Skeeter Corbin. I live on the corner. Are you looking for me?"

"And why would we be looking for you, Miss?"

"My husband hasn't come home, and I'm terribly worried. I thought maybe you..." But she doesn't complete the sentence because she can see the obvious in the policeman's expression. She then asks, "Is either of them here? Maybe they..."

The cop beckons her to accompany him into the other room. There she sees Hester slouched in a chair next to the computer with its screensaver of the cosmos. A broken old-fashion glass lies at her feet, and a faint odor of whiskey marks the air. Blood has crusted on one side of the older woman's head.

"She only came to this morning. She says her husband shot her last night."

The other cop is at the room's back wall, digging out the slug.

Hester reaches up and feels her wound, patting the circumference.

"We have an ambulance on its way, Mam."

Hester half-laughs and is about to make a disparaging remark about Faldowski, when she sees the worry on Skeeter's face. She shakes her head. "I heard you in the other room. I know what you're thinking. But I don't know. I suppose he could have." She nods at the computer. She tells them all to read what's on the monitor behind the screensaver.

The cop and Skeeter move closer to the computer and lower their heads.

"This sounds like he wanted to kill himself," the cop says after reading the words a couple of times.

Hester shakes her head again. "I guess he didn't take my advice."

With great effort, she turns her chair around so she, too, can read the words on the screen.

> *At 60, it seemed to Faldowski the principal*
> *objection to his entire adult life was he'd kept*
> *the gun away from his head.*

Once finished, she reaches across the desk for the mouse and selects a word.

"I told him he should bold it."

The cop reads the message again, noting her edit of the next-to-last word. He winces.

"That's when he turned the gun on me," Hester says. "Who knew it's what he was looking for all these years. I meant it as a joke."

COLD S.O.B.

Trettel and The Second disapproved of how I told the story—they said as much, even in front of the detective—but after they walked out of the interrogation room, Sipowitz lowered his specs. I think he knew which of us had it straight.

It was crazy Farnham who suggested we follow our guys to Rupp Arena in Lexington. He claimed he had a cousin who was a walk-on for the Kentucky Wildcats. Trettel, a political science major who kept urging us to call him "Boss," said he was all for it, which meant The Second would be too. Too-Neat Ty came along about then, heard the plan, and invited himself. As for me, I love hoops. No way I was staying behind.

As there were five of us and because it's a two-and-a-half-hour jaunt, Too-Neat Ty volunteered his wheels, a ride with a rear seat that could accommodate three people without each feeling up the other. Trettel stretched his long legs up front with Ty while the rest of us settled in the back.

I knew Ty since I was a little mother, and Farnham was something of a friend for most of that time. I say "something," because had he not lived on the same street, I might have avoided him completely. No doubt he lent me money on occasion for a soda or a Klondike, and there were probably a few childish favors done on my behalf. But at fourteen, when I watched him destroy a robin, I realized it was best to keep some distance. Mind, Farnham didn't just cause the poor bird's death. Rather, he used a shovel and smashed it to a pulp, then rolled out his old man's Lawn Boy for cleanup. And I say he "probably" did me a favor because it wasn't something for which you could ask. Anything along that line he viewed as an attempt to manipulate.

Too-Neat Ty, on the other hand, who lived in the opposite direction and on a dead-end street, became a friend of sorts only because his mother and mine worked at the Save-A-Lot. I wasn't the one to stick him with the handle, but it was accurate. The poor sonovabitch's shoes were always shined; seldom did he wear sneaks or even casual leather. His brown hair was full, like a fertilized bush, properly pruned throughout most every day of the year. There wasn't a zit on his face, not even when he hormoned to teen. An obscenity was foreign matter to his mouth.

Despite all this, there was an off-kilter streak in Ty. For example, when bungee jumping showed up on the scene as a daredevil thing to do for a rush, he took what bungee cords there were in his old man's tool shed and tied them together, then climbed a tree. Knotting one end of the cord around a thick limb, he held to the other and flung his ass into the air. Barely a third of the way down, he reached for a branch. A futile effort, as his weight shot him like a meteor straight through the foliage to Mother Earth, and he was just lucky his knees did not force themselves into his marshmallow of a skull like a couple of froze-up, oil-starved pistons.

On another occasion, he removed his old man's revolver from the gun case, shoved a single cartridge inside, spun the cylinder, and stuck it to the side of his head while gooning at me. Only the screwball couldn't force himself to pull the trigger.

Two sickos, Farnham and Ty. And with high school graduation I was expecting to be rid of them both. But it wasn't how matters turned out. Like myself they got enrolled at UT, and the three of us, incredibly, started hanging out together, joined soon by Trettel and The Second.

*

The trip to the game began in usual fashion. What I mean is, Farnham gave Ty the same warning he gave whenever the bunch of us were about to spend some concentrated time together.

"You keep the religion crap to a minimum," he said.

During the previous year Ty had become a born-again, and so he was always referencing the Lord and quoting Scripture. It was annoying, but at the same time he seemed to be an improved guy. Like maybe the days of the revolver and jumping out of trees were behind him.

"Praise God, you have my word, Farnham," Ty replied in the rearview mirror, catching the eye of each of us sitting in the back seat.

Of course, I knew other born-agains and some of these, when they were forced to promise restraint, had another thing at the back of their minds, which they didn't believe fell within the parameters of their pledge. Ty, it soon became apparent, was among this group. His deal was this: he intended to comment on every stupid adage and advice-to-live-by that was appearing this week on the front lawns of countless churches. He'd already remarked on two, including *"God doesn't promise a destination, only a soft landing"* and here was another.

"'What's missing?'" he read. *"'C–H–blank–blank–C–H..'* You get it, Farnham?"

"Yeah, I got it. What's missing is 'U R.'"

"No, my friend," said Ty, smiling into the rearview. "You are. I already go to church."

"Good for you," I said.

Farnham began to stare at the back of Ty's head, and he didn't widen his focus until the car swung onto the ramp for I-75 North. Fortunately, we would be church-free for a while and so I began to shoot the shit with Trettel about his political science class on U.S. hegemony. The Second said he couldn't wait to take the course himself because Trettel spoke real highly of the professor teaching it. I told the obedient shrimp, yeah, the dude was okay, as I once had the prof for a general course on government, but I added that he would still have to do the work. This prof, who weighed about a thousand pounds, didn't give any free passes no matter how often you agreed with him or laughed at his jokes.

A half-hour up the road, an exit appeared and Ty slowed the car.

"What's up?" Trettel asked.

"I need gas. And I could use a Mountain Dew."

There was an enormous brick-and-stone church with a copper-clad spire in the middle of a well-groomed field at the end of the exit. At the rear I could see three sets of swings and a couple of different-sized sliding boards for children. Out front was a sign.

"Hey Too-Neat," said Farnham. "Do you know that churches like this mega baby in front of us are nothing but one more American franchise, like a Hardee's or a Papa John's? More big business, that's all they are."

Ty glanced up in the mirror with a quizzical expression. "Oh, they are not."

"Trust me. Here's how it works. The parent company comes in and does all the research and demographics. It finds out how many Christians live nearby, the number who will attend services, how much tithing they'll accept, plus the number of vacationers who are likely to swing off the interstate for a visit, and so on. Some minister in need of a church can then buy in. He passes on seventy percent of the donations, but still is able to make a good living for himself. That's not all. A lot of the wear and tear on the church is maintained with the help of the parent company. If attendance drops, it'll even come back in with a construction team and redo some of the exterior and interior decorations to freshen things up. You know, like put up a new and bigger cross."

Ty again looked in the mirror, this time at The Second and myself. "Have either of you ever heard of anything like that?"

"Can't say I have," I said.

"I've never heard of it," said Trettel.

"Me neither," echoed The Second.

"Where did you learn of this?" Ty asked Farnham.

"Don't recall. But think about it. Think and tell me if you haven't seen another church this size right on the corner of an exit off an interstate. Prime real estate, and there's no taxes levied. It's a franchise. It wouldn't surprise me if they sell blessed hamburgers and fries in the basement."

We reached the end of the exit where there was a stop sign. Ty was forced to focus his attention on the intersection. Several cars and trucks with blinking signals were waiting to make a turn one direction or another. Farnham swung his head toward me and offered a faintly malevolent grin I'd seen before to let me know that he'd made up everything he'd just said.

When the intersection was clear, Ty turned left and drifted us past the church toward a convenience store with gas pumps out front. He looked over his shoulder briefly in order to read the words encased in a large marble box nearer the road than church.

"Now there's a proverb you can't argue with," he said.

The rest of us glanced over at the church to read the message: *"He who angers you controls you."*

"More crap," said Farnham.

Ty laughed to himself, but it was audible to the rest of us.

"I mean it," Farnham said. "It's crap."

Trettel turned around and said, "A junior and you're still using words like 'crap'?"

"I use words like 'tithing' too, or weren't you listening? Look, scuzzbucket! I know one of these days after you graduate you intend to run for political office. Well let me just say that if what I hear coming out of your mouth is crap, you rest assured that's what I'm going to call it."

"Hey, Boss isn't a scuzzbucket," said The Second. He was sitting between Farnham and myself.

"Shut your hole," Farnham said.

"I can't believe you talk like that," said Trettel. "I really can't."

Ty was again looking in the mirror at the three of us in back.

"I want to discuss that proverb," he said as he pulled into the lot of the convenience store and next to a pump. "After I fill up."

Trettel offered to get Ty his soda. The rest of us joined him.

Inside, at the cooler, Trettel confronted Farnham. "Why're you trying to get into an argument with Too-Neat?"

"Hey, he's the one pushing things. And that line out there on the church lawn isn't the almighty truism he thinks it is."

"Sounds true enough to me," said Trettel, grabbing a Dew for Ty and a Coke for himself from the cooler.

As the four of us left the store for the car, Ty was walking up to pay for the fill-up. Trettel checked the amount on the pump, and when Ty returned and slid behind the steering wheel, we each handed over some money for our share of the gas. A minute later we were back to rolling up the interstate. Sixty, seventy. Ty took the needle up to eighty and steadied it. Other drivers still passed us.

"Okay, let's get to it," Ty began. "Why do you regard those words of wisdom to be false? They strike me so true I can't believe anyone would think otherwise. Not even you, my rebellious friend."

I saw Trettel glance back at Farnham with the hope Farnham would let the matter drop, and it seemed he was willing. It was otherwise with Ty.

"Come on. Speak up. Perhaps you're becoming angry. Are you, Farnham? Perhaps my challenging your view is getting under your skin. And if that's the case, then I'm in control of your stubborn psyche, and everyone here knows it." Ty finished with another look in the mirror that framed a picture of a young man anticipating a small victory.

For a time Farnham stayed silent, peering out his window; and it appeared that Trettel, shooting a glance over his shoulder at The Second, was congratulating himself for persuading Farnham not to argue.

However, Farnham finally did speak. And the words came out a whisper.

"What if I'm controlling my anger?"

"What's that?" Ty asked.

And then, when Ty looked in the rearview, the self-satisfied grin still sitting on his smooth, unblemished mug, Farnham turned his own head and met him face-to-face. From what I could tell as I observed him from the side, Farnham didn't regard the matter underway as the least bit comical.

"I said, what if I'm controlling my anger?"

"Even so," Trettel began, but he shut himself down as I telegraphed a message that said, *What the hell are you doing? Wasn't it your idea for Farnham to shut up?*

Ty said, "I know what Trettel was about to say, and he's correct. If you control your anger on purpose, it's because you're under the influence of another human being. It's not something you would normally do. You're being reminded to be careful, not to let your anger get out of hand."

"You think so?" Farnham said.

"Don't you?"

Farnham's fingers started to dance on the buckle of his belt that looped around his waist and under a thin tire of flab. Ty kept switching his eyes between the interstate, which the car was rapidly gobbling up, and the mirror as he waited on a reply.

"Some people enjoy their anger," Farnham said, almost smugly. "They like getting to it, and getting to it quickly."

"Like who? Are you saying you do? I don't buy it. If you're becoming annoyed, it's because I'm in control."

Farnham unbuckled the belt and I expected him to open the top of his jeans as well. I had watched him do this routine numerous times in the past as a way to restore comfort to himself. The jeans were too old for the newly added fat around his twenty-year-old waist. Only this time the jeans remained buttoned, the zipper closed.

"You can't control me," he said.

"I can, and I am. Like it or not, I'm controlling you as we speak. It's obvious you're becoming upset with me. That means I'm the one calling the shots. *'He who angers you controls you.'"*

"No one controls me," Farnham said.

"My good friend, whether you agree or not, I am."

Perhaps I should have seen it coming, but although thoughts on these sick sons-of-bitches had run through my brain on many occasions when we were growing up, not once had I entertained the pair of them coming together to interact and how such a meeting might play out. When Farnham slipped the belt from its half-dozen loops, I realized too late what he was about to do, just as I realized with equal clarity that the rebirth of Too-Neat Ty was one not of spiritual renewal, but was instead a search for the inner peace he would need to complete what he had long wanted to do. And crazy Farnham, he decided, would serve as his revolver and bungee cord.

Wrapping the ends of the belt around each hand, Farnham jerked his body forward and looped the leather over the man sitting at his front as though the cowhide strip were a jump rope. Ty's head first shot backward against the headrest, then jolted upward as the belt tightened against his throat. His upper body rounded and expanded like a balloon about to burst, and the horrible gagging erupted. On its own the car careened sharply left, but was soon reeling all over the pavement, with no decrease in speed. The Second and I grabbed wildly at Farnham in an attempt to force his release of the leather belt, but he was strong from unchained insanity, surrendering not an inch; and Trettel, although he was in a position to perhaps wrestle a hand between the belt and Ty's throat and maybe disrupt the strangulation, directed his alarm at steering the car and bringing it to a stop. He succeeded with the first, but Ty's right leg remained pressed to the pedal at the same time the edge of his knee was locked against the key ring in the ignition, and no amount of effort from Trettel could move the leg at either point.

I remember looking in the mirror. Ty's eyes were wide open, bulging, draining of blood; but still they seemed to be looking at something off in the distance, imploring whatever it was to remain with him, to see this matter through and to not allow it to end like failures of the past. I too saw something, the truth of what was taking place. Neither of these sick bastards gave a damn if they killed the rest of us. And goddammit, my own anger flared.

I hauled back my right arm and, as though I were swinging a four-pound hammer, drove its fist past The Second into Ty's temple. That buckled the leg like it was water. The car slowed, and Trettel wrestled it to a stop in the grassy median.

The three of us were out of the car on our side and rushing to the other, but Farnham was out too and opening the driver's door. He reached in and dragged Ty out of the car by the collar and

132

F. E. Mazur

deposited him on the grass like he would a flattened wading pool. Ty was dead. We all knew it.

"My god," Trettel groaned, his head moving about like a tragic bobblehead.

A driver of another vehicle must have seen the reckless behavior of the car and phoned police because a smokey showed soon after, with several more close behind. Trettel told the cops what happened, with The Second backing him up, and Farnham, who was draining the remaining soda from Ty's can, made no attempt to deny their story, or change a single detail. When they asked me about it, I said everything the same. No one thought to ask why I'd hit Too-Neat Ty and not Farnham.

The police cuffed Farnham and pushed him toward one of their cars as the lights from it and the others continued to flash.

"Looks like Too-Neat wasn't in control like he thought," he said to me.

The Second, in earshot, cried, "You're not even sorry, you sonovabitch!"

To me Farnham whispered, "I'm sorry it wasn't the fuckhead who wrote that stupid line."

He knew I was the only one of us three at whom he might attempt to give a grin of satisfaction arising from the belief he had proven his point, and when the cop wasn't looking our way he did. I wasn't going to tell him the truth. That Ty convinced himself he had formed a special pact with God who would keep him in control once he decided to end his life. Instead, I half-smiled back and muttered so only he could hear, "I think probably the only thing you're apologizing for, you nutty bastard, is that you forgot to bring along the Lawn Boy."

An hour later at the police station, in the interrogation room before fat-ass Sipowitz, or whatever his name was, entered and shut the door, we sat silently around the table, the three of us, until The Second dared to mutter: "You hit him in the head really hard."

What he was implying surprised me coming from him, but it hadn't escaped my own thoughts. And although I could have

133

argued Farnham's position on anger and control, in regard to myself I would be forced by honesty to argue Ty's.

I met The Second's eyes, wondering just how far his daring would go, but the answer for certain wasn't in them, and he knew this as well. After a while, we both looked at Trettel. That moment in time I learned that Trettel already knew there was political value to silence and omission. If I was the actual cause of death of Too-Neat Ty, some medical examiner would have to bring it to light. "Boss" Trettel wasn't going to say anything more to the police than he already had.

DOREEN'S SNOOZELEN

Pap comes home from work, carrying a bag. Mom is the first to ask.

"Feesh," says Pap.

"Fish? You hate fish. Every time I make it, you complain."

Pap holds the bag up to his craggy face, shakes it a tiny little, and grins.

My twin sister Doreen says, "What sort of fish worth eating fits into a bag that small?"

"Bingo!" says Pap. "These feesh aren't for eating. These feesh are for looking at. Find me one of those glass blocks I brought home from a gravesite," he says to Mom. "They need to get into something bigger with more water, else they'll die."

He opens the brown paper bag and slides out a clear plastic one bulging with air and three inches of water. At the bottom seam two little fish begin jerking about and climbing over each other's dorsal as though some celebrity of their own, like Charlie the Tuna, has just appeared outside their new window.

Ricky sees what I expect him to see and he pantomimes an explosion of the inflated bag between his small hands, like it's an empty potato chip one. Never too sure about Ricky, Pap draws the fish closer to himself, out of my son's reach.

"Here," he says, moving to the kitchen sink. "Look at them under this fluorescent light where the red and blue really show up."

"Oh my, are they ever pretty," croons Doreen, who's pretty herself.

"They're tropicals. Neon tets they're called."

Ricky reaches for the bag and Pap slaps his hand. "They're for looking at," he repeats sternly.

Ricky, already making the face, turns to Doreen and me and with slow exaggeration, even resembling that big-lipped Channing actress who Mom used to talk about after seeing the only Broadway show she's ever seen, mouths Pap's words: *They're for LOOOOK-ing at.* Barely four, you wouldn't think the little shit would do such a thing.

Mom asks why Pap has brought home tropical fish when we don't have an aquarium, and Pap says that Jasky stopped off at a pet store to pick up some special food he'd ordered for his miniature schnauzer. Nowadays, Mom's usually too exhausted to press anything and she accepts his explanation without saying another word, although I can't see where he's answered her question.

*

Pap began working for Jasky last Thanksgiving. It's his second job and although it pays better than his regular employment as the groundskeeper at the cemetery, the hours aren't always much. What Pap does is solder tiny electronic parts onto a circuit board that becomes a switch.

"The switches are added to products already on the market," Jasky explained to the rest of us the first time he came by to pick up Pap in his truck. "The reason I modify these products is so people with severe disabilities and poor motor control can use them." He glanced at Ricky when he said this and Doreen believes this was intentional. She later explained that Jasky most likely had read the graffiti we went searching for before Ricky's birth, but never discovered. She told me also what she's always expected that graffiti to say. The rest I figured for myself, which is Jasky thinks it's only a matter of time until my son exhibits the signs of a mental retard.

Jasky operates his small business in the carpeted basement of a shoe store, and Pap can go inside at any time because he has a key and knows the code to shut off the alarm. Besides Pap, Jasky employs Mildred who keeps the books, fills orders, runs the Dirt Devil, and does whatever other jobs crop up. The schnauzer, bored with spending his time below ground, usually snoozes near the bottled water, showing he's alive only when someone fills a paper cone and the big air bubble wobbles to the top with an emphatic "GO-LUB!"

One day when school was cancelled because of a bomb threat, Pap took me with him for more than just another visit. This time I would learn to solder. "It's another thing you'll know how to do, and it may come in handy some day like it has for me."

When later he disappeared into the toilet, Jasky sidled over and watched as I handled the soldering gun. He's a big glob of a man with thinning white hair, and he has that suspicious kind of fleshy Jell-O rippling across the face and down through his neck into his body to cause a person to wonder seriously about his private life with its secrets. I connected my completed switch with alligator clips to a stand-up panel with pictures of different foods, and the red lights above each picture went on one after another in a timed sequence.

"What do you think of this boy, Mildred? Only thirteen years old when he got his first piece. I had to wait until I was twenty."

"I'm sure you did," said Mildred.

"Now what's that supposed to mean?"

"Handsome man like you, Ed, you probably couldn't decide which female would be the lucky first, and so the years slipped by."

"How old were you?"

"That's none of your business."

"I was what they call a 'late bloomer.' I didn't even experience my first ejaculation until I was seventeen, and I was asleep when it happened."

"And your right hand has rarely enjoyed a night's rest since, isn't that right?"

"You're worse than I am, Mildred."

Mildred winked and smiled at me.

"When this early bloomer's father gets back from the john, I want to show you all some new things I'm considering adding to our product line. We might even do a small catalog." He reached over my shoulder and pressed the switch I'd made. The lights stopped their sequential blinking and the one under the milkshake stayed lit. "Good job, Jerry," he said.

137

Neither Pap nor Jasky is aware that Mildred and I previously met, and my growth over the past four years has apparently morphed my appearance enough that Mildred has forgotten more than just my name. Which is fine. The wink-and-a-smile was her way of letting me know she talked the way she had because dealing with Jasky requires it. It's the two photographs on exhibit beside her computer that made me think this. The person in both is her son. In the first picture the boy is about Ricky's age, while in the other he is ten at most. In each his mouth is open wide, like a traumatized cat's, and the wet tongue floats at the front as though he's tossed his liver. The day I had sex with Trisha, which produced Ricky, Mildred had him strapped in on the passenger side.

When Pap emerged from the toilet, drying his hands with a brown paper towel, Jasky waved him and me over to Mildred and her computer. He handed her a DVD to slip into the machine, an encyclopedia, he said, of just about every product available for the impaired and disabled. Jasky stated the item of interest and Mildred found it.

"What is that?" I asked when the second item flashed on the screen.

"That's the Peabody Picture Vocabulary Test," Mildred informed me.

It was little more than a book with a plastic ring binder at the top.

"I've ordered easels from my supplier to position it at a somewhat vertical angle," Jasky said to Pap. "We'll attach some lights to the frame to correspond with the picture matrix, then make a switch that will allow the lights to scan."

After explaining, Jasky shifted his attention from Pap to me, and a grin appeared, like he knew something but wasn't going to come right out and say he knew. I interpreted this to mean he thought Doreen and I would become familiar in a very short time with this test and his addition of scanning lights, the latter obviously to be used with kids and others who are unable to speak

138

and identify the items in the pictures. But Ricky *can* talk, except he rarely does, which is something Jasky doesn't know. And I realized then that Ed Jasky is, at one and the same time, a very smart sonovabitch and a very dumb sonovabitch; because on the latter, although we never had much to do with him before Pap began the soldering, he nonetheless passed through the neighborhood enough to have seen Doreen on the porch watering Mom's hanging plants, or sunning out in our postage-stamp yard, my smidgen of a fraternal twin who, if she ever does become pregnant, will resemble a baby hippo. There's no chance she will be the kind who "doesn't show."

"We'll have to come up with a name for each new item," he said, losing the grin. "Any ideas for this one? Nothing fancy. Just something to identify it and the modification we'll make. Think about it for the catalog, okay?"

The rest of the items were to require switches too, including a Polaroid camera that Jasky said children with Down's Syndrome would be able to use.

Mildred then surfed through a few additional screens. At one I asked her to back up because I hadn't seen a product.

"The entire room is the product," she said, and she clicked on the small picture that enlarged to fill the screen, and the motion and accompanying sound were eerily soothing.

"It's sensory stimulation in the form of lights, textures and acoustical tones that, together, provide a comforting environment," said Jasky, like he was reading from an advertisement. "Snoozelen. That's what it's known as in the field. Costs a bundle to install. Mildred has some first-hand knowledge about it and can tell you more than I can."

I let Mildred be while I studied the Snoozelen on my own. All the furniture looked like bean bags that were given shape. The light filling the room was of many different colors—soft, nothing harsh—and it stretched and ebbed, like I've heard about the northern lights, crawling faintly, even creepy-like, across the walls. In the corners large transparent tubes, tinted yellow, blue, pink and green, ran from floor to ceiling, and inside them air circulated through water providing the dominant sound, a broken but ongoing patter of gurgling bubbles, streaming upward. Doreen and I once watched some television re-runs of an old show Pap used to enjoy called *Sea Hunt*, which took place mostly underwater, and the only sounds heard were the breathing of the divers; the only light seen, the chopped rays from the sun above the surface. Everything in that program had seemed to be in slow motion, and the effect on both of us was to lie back and do nothing. I thought the Snoozelen would probably encourage the same.

"There's nothing there requires solder," Pap said to me.

"I'm sure he can see that," Jasky said, and he put a hand on Pap's shoulder as a signal it was time to resume the building of more switches.

*

This Trisha I've mentioned was seventeen at the time I had my first sex, and although a person is expected to remember all the details about their first sexual experience, to say I know how it happened would be a mostly invented story. She now attends an expensive all-girls college several states away while her parents continue to live in a wealthy housing tract not far from the local community park. The roads running through the development were newly paved four years ago and they have turns and dips, as the tract isn't squared off, nor was it gated as it is now. It was a great place for us kids to ride our bikes and skateboards.

This Trisha had owned a mysterious reputation and it attracted a group of us who made sure our route to and from the development passed her house, which is the largest and rests on a slope overlooking the others.

We saw her outside only once, and it was toward evening. An older and bolder friend of mine at the front of our bicycle convoy called to her. She sashayed down to the street in a pair of tight white jeans, taking her good old time, her long black hair swishing this way and that. I was at the rear and never uttered a word, the

140

reason she insisted I stay once the others pedaled off toward home. A few moments later, a car appeared from the rear of the house and drifted down the driveway with the window on the driver's side all the way open. She introduced the two of us right away, adding that Mildred was their housekeeper. She had to ask for my name. Mildred's boy, she ignored. Once the car was gone, she curled her fingers around the handlebars and while climbing backwards, tugged the bike and me up the driveway, allowing the front tire to roll through her crotch.

Inside the fancy house we were alone, not even a dog or cat around, and as a friend of mine from school likes to say stupidly upon every surprise in his life, *Vi-ola!* Jerry Menard had his first sex.

When her parents eventually realized she was pregnant, they went off like a fire hydrant struck by a car, but all the more so after she told them I was the father and they learned I was but thirteen years old. Her own father, a big, big, B-I-G honcho with the electric company, refused to believe it. Even after Ricky was born, he paid for me to take a test to prove the fact I was, not wasn't. The day he came to the house he informed our family he had no interest in being the "grandfather to a child who's the offspring of a gravedigger's son." Pap politely said he was a groundskeeper, not a gravedigger, but it made no impression.

Mom then asked him, "Are you forcing your poor daughter to abort the baby?"

"We're a moral family," he replied, as if Mom had insulted him. "Of course we're not going to kill the baby. Trisha will be delivered of the child and then surrender it for adoption."

"What about our son?"

"He's still a kid, for godsakes. He'll do the same to someone else's daughter if you and your husband don't get a leash on him." "Then what about us?" said Pap.

And Mom said, "Being grandparents to your daughter's child, we would like that."

He shook his head in a manner that said, "No way," and it

angered me that he thought so terribly little of Pap and Mom, and Doreen and myself. To him we were dirt, slime, absolute trash, and to make as certain as possible that nobody would associate his own with us, he was intending to sign my child over to some couple who lived far, far away.

"He'll put his name to paper!" Doreen boldly up and said. "We all will."

He interpreted this to mean we would hook up with a lawyer and fight the adoption.

"Surely you realize I have many more resources than you," he said, confronting Pap. "I can have my attorney drag this out till you've squandered every dollar you have saved, and the court still won't award the child to you."

"He'll sign a paper that says he won't ever reveal Trisha is the mother. But if not, then he'll start telling everyone right away that he is. And so will I! We'll tell it to all our classmates, all our teachers, everyone. I'll even personally write it on the bathroom wall of the girls' room at school."

His head swung slowly left like a motorized spotlight on a penitentiary tower as he suddenly realized Doreen was the family member he should be addressing, not Pap. And he didn't need to ponder the consequences of her threat for very long before buying into it.

*

When Doreen and I return from school, Mom is upset. The neon tets are dead. She discovered them on the floor. Pap says fish often jump out of containers, that he should have found a lid for the glass block formerly used for keeping candles burning at the breezy hillside cemetery; but Pap is covering for my son, not because he believes Ricky needs a break, but because Mom does. Because Mom, who is home all day, everyday, with my boy, needs hope this countless small disaster is of another's making, and that her grandson is not on course to become the criminal who will deserve every finger pointed his way. Yet I know the fish are dead because of Ricky. I know he belly-smacked his tiny hands into the block and tormented the little creatures by chasing them back and forth in the narrow container until they chose the only escape route possible, up and over its lip. I am certain, too, my son made no effort to save them, to scoop them up off the linoleum and drop them back into the water, that he fell onto his knees and watched them die slowly, that he most likely lowered his head to within inches of one and stared into its tiny eye until the gill behind lay still.

"Why did you bring them home in the first place?" Mom demands. "And you give me more than what you did the last time, or so help me!"

"A salesman at the store saw me looking at them while waiting for Ed," Pap says gently, aware that today Mom teeters on the edge. "He asked how they made me feel. I said watching them made me feel relaxed. And he said that's the very reason many people display feesh in their homes. He said they find it calms them down after a hectic day at work or whatever."

"And you thought...?"

"No. Not you or me. For him."

My son, for all the trouble he is, is not a dummy. He is aware he's the subject of his grandfather's talk; however, he will grow into a man who will not care what others say about him, whether good or bad. He will hear their words, but none will ever matter, and that's because other people will never matter to him. Not even me.

"I was mistaken, thinking the feesh alone," Pap says, his head shaking from disappointment. "I don't know what I was thinking."

*

Besides being the good-looking twin, Doreen's the smarter. "She just got the better egg," Mom liked to say before Ricky's arrival, while Pap, pretending this was an important moment in the battle of the sexes, would laugh and counter with "Pretty sure of yourself, woman, aren't you?" Our English teacher told the class that Doreen is able to *intellectualize* the world. What I think this means is, we can look at the same thing, and while others and myself will see what's there, my sister will see what isn't—and yet really is. It's not a simple idea to grab onto and explain, and I can feel the envy inside, along with regret that she and I did not develop from a single egg.

Although Doreen herself had yet to have sex, she knew at once the first time I did, and she asked a few questions about the experience and wanted to know with whom. After I told her, she made me promise not to boast to my friends and reveal Trisha's identity, which is the reason I was later surprised that she threatened to do exactly that to her father. Of course she'd realized very quickly that Mr. Big Electric Executive wasn't so worried about his daughter as he was about himself.

There never was a document to be signed that would have forbidden me to reveal the name of Ricky's mother. Although Doreen had introduced the idea, she's the only one of the family who really didn't expect such a thing to happen. By the following morning she had it all figured, and on our way to school I listened to her explanation. Trisha's father, in spite of his regard for our family as low-lifes, would trust our word not to spread anything, she said. She also predicted it would be otherwise with him. When I asked what she meant, she said I could find out for myself over the weekend.

So on Saturday morning she shouted me awake and after breakfast, we rode off on our bikes. The places we visited, to my complete disgust, were men's toilets. She said I was to read whatever graffiti was on their walls. Most I entered, or the two of us together. A few she dared advance into alone when I crabbed what we were doing was nuts. We must have visited the john of every convenience store and fast-food restaurant operating in our area, but came up empty. There were only the usual scribbled messages, and they meant nothing to me. I'd had enough and told her so.

"We're doing something wrong," she said. "Do you know

what it is?"

"I don't even know what I'm looking for because you won't tell me. I know only it has something to do with Trisha's jerk of a father. But do you think he ever eats at a fast-food joint?"

"Hey, you're right," she said, her face lighting up. "We've been exploring the wrong places." And for a moment I thought maybe my egg wasn't so bad after all, but in the end I figured my knowing something Doreen didn't was just a fluke.

And so next we headed out to the rich golf country club known as Sugar Bush, which spreads across the flats east of town and is overlooked by the cemetery where Pap works. The club seemed to provide scrubbed and fancy restrooms in just about every corner and down every hallway, as though people who are much better off than most of us can't wait very long once they get the call. Doreen and I checked the walls and stalls of each. Again we discovered nothing. Of course, there are other places where the area's wealthy hang out and Doreen wanted to persist with the search. But by this time I'd really had enough and started for home.

Doreen, too, reluctantly surrendered that day and went home with me, but it was certainly not the end to her quest. She would continue into the following year to visit the area's numerous men's rooms, even revisiting most because of the possibility that either of us might have overlooked "it." Still, in spite of her perseverance, which sometimes included a disguise using a piece or two of my clothing, she never found what she was seeking. Neither would she say what she was expecting to find, although this unwillingness may have been keyed to her age of thirteen when she was not inclined to swear, the reason she wanted me to see for myself. At seventeen there was no such reluctance, and when Jasky provided the cue in the form of a questionable glance at Ricky, she finally let out.

"*'Jerry Menard fucks his twin sister.'* That's what's written on the wall of a toilet somewhere in this town, Jerry. And Trisha's old man is the one who wrote it!"

If I gave the smallest hint of a response, it didn't show, and Doreen was expecting one.

"You don't believe he would do such a terrible thing, do you?" she said. "You think because he wears a suit every day, lives in that rich house and drives a big fancy car, that writing a thing like that on a restroom wall is beneath him. Well, Jerry, writing it on a wall at a dozen locations would be beneath him. Scratching it on a single wall where others just like himself will see it isn't the least beneath him."

It remained a stretch. "That's all we really know about him and it isn't much," I said.

"We know more than you think. Look at Trisha. She's in her last year of college. Four years she's been away from her father."

"What's that prove?"

"Has she ever called you once, or written a letter, asking about Ricky? It's not like she couldn't do it without her father knowing."

"Oh," was all I could say, as I understood what she was getting at.

"You know, too, Jerry, I think I gave him the idea when I threatened to write it on the walls at school. He wasn't worried about how uncomfortable and embarrassing that would be for his daughter. He was worried that one of us might write it where the kind of people with whom he hangs out would see it. And that's the reason he didn't wait to put out a little graffiti on his own. It's like he figured if he planted the seed, Ricky's birth would serve as the proof to others that the statement was correct."

Perhaps I am gullible, but it still remained hard to believe that a wealthy man, as he is, would ever take time out of his day to scratch something horrible on the wall of a men's john, realizing, surely, that he might even be caught in the defacing act. Still, I half-smiled to give her something.

"Someday, you'll run across it when you're not expecting," she said.

"Or you," I said.

"I'm too old to enter your restrooms. Someday, Jerry, you'll look up when you're finished doing your business, and it'll be on the wall right before your eyes."

*

On the street at the front of the house there's commotion. Mom and I go to the door, open it, peer out. Pap and Jasky are standing at the rear of Jasky's pickup, both working hard to release a jammed tailgate, while Jasky's schnauzer is scampering wildly from one yard to another, barking madly in the process. "Stay out of the street!" he shouts at it. Mom, displaying a worried face, follows the little dog with her eyes. I'm suddenly anxious for Mom. In the bed of the pickup sits an aquarium; it's rather large. The gate finally yields and Jasky starts to pull on it. Pap points to its support stand.

"You're right," says Jasky. "This tank weighs a ton. No sense putting it down, only to lift it again."

They slide the wooden stand off the truck bed and carry it toward the house. It's heavy, too, made obvious by their fast walk and shortened steps that cause them both to look a little sissified. When Pap sees me, he indicates with his head there are other things, smaller items in the pickup, to be brought in. He doesn't look at Mom as he and Jasky pass through the open door and disappear inside.

From around the corner of the house come Doreen and Ricky. I am already at the bed of the truck, searching for the other things. They've been tossed willy-nilly into several cardboard boxes: hood, pump, tubing, a fluorescent bulb, several bags of gravel, a filter of some kind, some fake plants, a plastic tall ship with a hole in its hull and broken masts, plus there's a bucket containing a thermometer, tube connectors, a bottle of some chemical to remove chlorine from the water, and other odds and ends.

Doreen stops next to me and looks at the various items in the boxes. Ricky is watching the frenetic schnauzer. Pap and Jasky reappear, and I now notice that my father is wearing a smile.

"What are you waiting for?" he says. "Grab a box and take it

147

into Ricky's room."

I offer to replace him with myself for hauling the heavy aquarium inside.

"Then you take Ed's end," he says. "Give him a break."

I scramble onto the bed and step among the boxes to get behind the aquarium.

"Fifty-five gallons," Pap says, beaming. "It's used, as is the rest of the stuff. But the storeowner swore it's all in good shape, right Ed?"

"I've known him a long time. He wouldn't gyp a soul."

Doreen is staring through a window on the cab with one eye on Ricky, who continues to stare at the schnauzer.

"Is there a net?"

"You don't need a net, Doreen," says Pap. "You just take those bags with the feesh and float them in the tank until the water temperatures are the same. Then open the bag and the feesh swim out."

"I think he did throw in a net," Jasky says to my sister as he opens the door on the cab. "It might be in that box with the hood."

Jasky reaches inside and pulls out one of the bags containing fish. "Hey, little Ricky," he calls. "You can help too. After all, these are for you."

Jasky holds out the bag and Ricky turns his attention away from the dog and approaches, almost suspiciously, his eye on Jasky as much as on the plastic bag.

"Go on. Take it inside."

Jasky reaches out and grabs my son's hand. He places the bag in it, then grabs the other hand and folds it over the first.

"Rick-_eeee_...," says Doreen, her second syllable a slow rise.

My son elevates his arms to the heavens, then dashes the bag to the ground. It's only luck it doesn't break.

"Well now..." says Jasky, making a face of stretched-out muscle as he lowers his head and looks away like someone who wonders why he ever involved himself in a matter.

"When everything's set up, he won't do that," says Pap. "So

148

let's get at it. These things can't stay in these bags forever."

Before lifting my end of the aquarium, I shift my gaze to the doorway to read Mom's reaction. Only she's disappeared.

*

Ricky's windowless bedroom at a back corner of the house is the smallest, and the aquarium seems even bigger than it actually is. It dominates the space, especially once it is filled with water, the plastic plants and two dozen fish are added, the tiny pump is pushing countless bubbles of air through six transparent tubes extending from what Pap informed everyone is an underground filter, and the fluorescent light under the chrome hood is switched on. The inch-long neon tets—this time there are eight—school from one end of their new environment to the other, their colors brilliant under the light, as are the pink and white gravel and the green artificial flora. And the room itself glows softly.

This could work, I think. And Pap, I can see, has recaptured his smile since the incident earlier involving Jasky. Even Mom seems hopeful, as she positions herself so that Ricky, already dressed for bed, does not see that she is submerging a hand into the aquarium to move the tall ship with the broken masts among the plants and on its side where the gaping hole of its hull becomes of immediate interest to the tets.

"It's supposed to be a sunken ship, so it should look like one," she says to the rest of us.

As a finishing touch, Doreen brings in several pillows from elsewhere in the house and pushes them together on the throw rug in front of the aquarium. Then she leads Ricky over and sets him down among them. The only sound is the quiet, reassuring hum of the air pump and the bubbling aeration coming from inside the glass tank. I'm feeling optimistic, we all are, it's on our faces, except Doreen's remains all business, and Ricky's … well, my son's looks are often a mystery.

"We'll just have to wait and see," says Pap. "Let's leave him alone for the rest of the evening. And Doreen, since you're always the last person in this house to go to bed, will you look in and turn out the light in the hood?"

*

Early in the night the need to relieve myself gets me up. I leave my room for the hall and the bathroom at one end. But at the opposite end, there is light seeping from under the door on Ricky's bedroom. The rest of the house is dark so that I can only conclude Doreen went to bed, forgetting what Pap asked her to do, although that would be very unlike her. First I pee, then pad down to where I hope my son is sleeping. I push gently on the door.

Still lounging among the pillows, Ricky remains awake, his eyes fixed on the glowing aquarium, inside of which there is not a fish to be seen.

A strange thought strikes me. *My four-year old son has eaten all his fish, swallowed them whole.*

I tiptoe over to the aquarium. He doesn't shift his attention the least from it to his father. Are all the tropicals hiding inside the damaged hull of the ship, where it is dark and where they can avoid his penetrating gaze?

No. The fish, simply, are gone, and yet I am relieved not to see any of them lying dead around my feet, although there are a few tiny pools of water that keep me from enjoying my relief completely. Leaning against the rear of the stand is the net. I reach down to touch its mesh and discover it is wet.

"They're next to my bed," I hear Doreen say in a hush. She's behind me, at the door. "I put them in a bucket. I'm taking them to school tomorrow. To the biology room."

When I turn to look at her, I see that she is staring at Ricky even though she's speaking to me.

"Pap—" I begin to say.

"Pap means well, but he's wrong, Jerry. He would have destroyed them all. This is better. This will accomplish what Pap wanted in the first place. This will give Mom some relief. Have you looked at him? Look at his jammies. He's wet to the shoulders."

Ricky is, I can see that now. Both sleeves are sopped with water, and on the pillow beneath each arm is a widening circle of dampness.

"They were dry when I removed the fish," she says quietly, at the same time now looking at me because it is clear there is more contained in what she has said, and she wants me to realize what it is. Try as I do, I'm unable. It's the two eggs again.

She raises her whisper a notch, for emphasis. "Look at him closely, Jerry. Look at his eyes!"

I do as she says and stoop, getting almost directly in front of my boy's line of vision. The eyes are wide open and they are cycling. The things they track are the unending bubbles shifting and bumping against the insides of the tubes as they rush to the surface. From bottom to top, and back to bottom, that's the movement of my son's eyes.

"He tried to kill them, Jerry. He didn't know. I'll explain to Pap in the morning. But it's going to be all right."

Still, something—I don't know what it is—worries me as I watch the eyes of my son continue to cycle. I can hope only that soon enough it will worry my sister as well.

SOMALIA

As became her habit, Crystal derided me. She said I could never understand our summer neighbor.

"What is there to understand?" I rejoined. "The man walks around with blinders on."

"Mr. Positive" was how I addressed Carl if I was feeling pleasantly nasty. Florence wasn't any different. I won't say she was like one of those irritatingly nutant reporters on everybody's local news, unconsciously yes-ing her silver-haired head to the ridiculous word or two her husband delivered as he responded to my criticism of the nation's deplorable social mores, or questions about a government policy doomed to fail; but her facial expressions, a mix of kindergarten optimism and Mother T beatitude, displayed too often the look of *"All is well."* Taking the poor woman seriously could exact a price.

Carl, who each summer wore a new baseball cap advertising some local business and whose dark fissures crisscrossed his face like more a map of a thousand hyperlinks than old leather, had three decades on me. It was half this amount of time that passed following our marriage before Crystal and I purchased the splendid log cabin, formerly owned by a state senator, which sat next to theirs. Before Crystal left, the four of us got together in the mountains each August, along with their two grandsons. Within that first year of ownership, a sinkhole developed on the boundary separating our properties and, following an all-day deluge, a pond formed. Inquiring of the people at Cooperative Extension, Carl learned that a thick stratum of clay lay underneath parts of the region, and I went along with getting a bulldozer in to widen and deepen the hole. Carl's pitch was we would all go swimming afterwards, plus if a couple buckets of panfish and some smallmouth bass (my vote was for the largemouth, just to be contrary) were stocked, we could become anglers and enjoy the tasty delights of a fresh catch well into the future. But he was thinking really of the boys, who soon would demonstrate they loved both water activities. And perhaps he was betting that Crystal and I still might have children one day who would appreciate a pond with dimensions larger than a kiddy pool.

To my knowledge Carl never once entered the water, except to stick a finger in to take its temperature. Neither can I recall a time, not even one of those *grandfather-teaches-grandson* occasions, when he cast out a line. Truth be told, I did little more. Mostly we visited at each other's shaded picnic table during hot afternoons and the cooler evenings: Carl bringing the pre-WWII Voigtlander and his beer, four cans minimum; me, my frosted tumbler and a pitcher of iced tea. Sometimes Florence joined us, and when Crystal was around, so would she, first spraying her long beautiful legs with some Avon fragrance that doubled as a bug repellent. Still, usually, it was just Carl and myself.

However, during those years when the wives did amble over, Carl often would announce that the two of us had been solving world problems.

"Well, that's good," you could count on Florence saying. "The world can always stand improvement."

One afternoon I felt it time to correct Mr. Positive in the presence of his wife. "I'm the one attempting to solve the problems, dear lady. Not this old fart of a hubby of yours."

"And what was Carl doing, Mitch?" my Crystal asked.

Hell, Carl was doing what he'd always done. Ask the toughest question about an education or financial bill that you know is folly, Carl would smile. Blast some public official deserving of more than harsh criticism, like maybe thirty years at hard labor—or even a bullet I once said to him and Florence just to shake 'em up (and it did Florence, believe me it did!)—Carl could be expected to toss in a sideways nod to go with the smile. When this old man spoke, it did not amount to much, and I always felt like scratching my head, although I never did so in front of him or Florence. In front of them I usually rubbed my chin. Still, the thought was there, *What a goddamn imbecile!*

During the last summer the four of us were at camp, the hot issue under regurgitation by the liberal airways was greater taxation of the wealthy, and I got into it with Carl because he favored the idea.

"Equal treatment, that's all I'm asking for, Carl. When you treat me equally, you treat me fairly. You should be insisting on the same. The numbers left of the decimal should not be a factor."

"What about those men and women who aren't your equal, Mitch?"

"There's quite a few who aren't my equal. Just how does that figure into tax rates?" I challenged him.

No spoken response from old Carl. Just the expected sip from the beer can, the smile, then that trademark sideways nod.

For once I decided to play the game back. I took a long drink of my iced tea and smiled too. Carl, I was certain, did not have the resources to equal mine, yet his summer camp, which must have set him back a hundred and fifty grand even years ago when inflation had been hardly a concern, was evidence he nonetheless had plenty. Did he work for it? Not likely! The man was union throughout his working days, and anyone who's even remotely honest with himself knows that union wages are paid out on the basis of contract, not merit. However, I wasn't intending to say the same to Carl. Quite the contrary. Aware as I am now, as I was then, that the union man believes he has earned his money, I

155

played the role of a sycophant.

"Carl, you put in long hours and did whatever was required to get where you are today. You've worked hard for your money. I know that. Well, so have I. I worked hard to get the big bucks, and today I work my investments just as hard. So why should either one of us be forced to pay more tax because we labored with greater industry than the rest? You tell me that, Carl my friend."

I had him by his senior citizen's balls and he knew it. He asked Crystal if she wanted a beer.

"No thanks, Carl," she said, then ran him some interference. "Are the bugs bothering you? Stick out your leg."

"Carl," I said, knocking once on the picnic table. "The bugs can wait. Pay attention."

"Mitch, you know I didn't make my money in Somalia," he said. "You know that, don't you?"

"Somalia?" I cannot imagine what the look on my face must have been, but it did not discourage Carl.

"Yes, Somalia," he repeated. "I didn't make it in Darfur or Bangladesh either."

Does he know that Darfur isn't even a goddamn country? I remember thinking while looking at the darkening sky. And then I began to laugh. I couldn't help myself. And if it was embarrassing to Carl and his devoted Florence, they had only him to blame for responding so stupidly. I looked to Crystal and, maybe because it was a most pleasant evening with a yellow half-moon rising above the pines, she wrapped an arm around my shoulders and began to laugh too. What I was hoping for, then, was that, for once, she had seen how asinine our neighbor could be.

"Hold it right there," Carl said. He picked up the Voigtlander, brought the eyepiece to his right eye, and tripped the shutter and flash. "That's going to be one great picture of you two lovebirds."

Carl was never right about any subject we ever discussed, except maybe the pond, and he did not explain his "Somalia" remark that evening if, in fact, there was anything to explain. But, as I know a little something about photography, I must say the old

156

man could take a good picture. He was right about the snapshot.

One day after I found Crystal's departure note attached to the computer monitor at home, the color photo arrived in the mail. As a couple, we never looked better, never happier. Even the photos in our wedding album could not compete.

And it gave me an idea. I thought if Crystal could see this photo, she might appreciate what it was saying about us, what it was showing we were capable of as a married couple. I decided to send her an eight-by-ten, the moment I learned where she was living.

I telephoned Carl. Florence answered.

"He's not here, Mitch.... Yes, we thought it was a wonderful photo of Crystal and you."

"Look, tell Carl, when he gets in," I told her, "to put the picture's negative in an envelope and drop it in the mail. I want to order an enlargement."

"Carl doesn't ever keep the negatives. He throws them away as soon as he receives the prints."

So much for that idea, I thought, and I said the same to Florence.

"I'm sorry, Mitch," she said.

I didn't think the smaller picture would have the same effect on Crystal as it had on me. I set it aside with some things on my desk that were later thrown out. It's not shown itself since.

*

Once Crystal was gone from my daily life, I might have imagined the months ahead would pass slowly. They did not. Another August appeared on the calendar without my awareness that summer was halfway over, and I made the decision to travel out to the camp alone, yet with a vague hope she would make an appearance. Because the log cabin was well equipped, the cupboards seldom bare, and a versatile wardrobe occupied the closet, I needed merely to get in the car, once I was sure Carl and Florence would be there, and make the drive. About the only thing

157

to accompany me was a digital camera that I'd purchased online a month before.

The first evening they both came out of their camp and walked over to join me at the picnic table. Florence didn't hesitate to inquire where Crystal was, and so I told Carl and her that I was now alone.

"I'm so sorry, Mitch," Florence said. Carl bunched his lips.

"It's okay," I said. "All right, it's not really okay, but what's a guy to do?"

"What *are* you going to do?" Florence asked.

"Take pictures," I replied, hoping to keep the moment on the upbeat. "Beginning with you guys. Come on, Florence, scooch on over closer to your lesser half."

She did so after I fluttered my hand several times. Carl inclined his head toward her and she did the same.

Florence slid back on the bench to her former spot after I pushed the button.

"Are you thinking of selling the place?" she asked.

"Is that what you're worried about? Who you might get for a new neighbor?"

"It was just a question," Carl said. He pointed to his four-pack. I waved it off.

"I thought you might finally be ready," he said.

"We've always liked both Crystal and you very much, Mitch," Florence said. "Your announcement just has us wondering, that's all."

"Did you ever think she would leave me?"

"It's not our place," Florence said, shaking her head.

I guffawed. "Not your place? That only means you have something to say! So say it!"

Carl grimaced, offended, apparently, by my tone.

Florence spread her arms and laid one hand on his, the other on mine.

I softened my voice to match her touch. "What is it, Florence? We didn't all meet a week ago."

"Because we're friends. Remember that."

I surrendered the nod she wanted.

"You're much smarter than the rest of us, Mitch. I've always known you were more intelligent than me, and Carl, too, would acknowledge you have it over him, wouldn't you, Carl? You had it over Crystal as well. I never said that to her out of concern I might hurt her feelings."

"It's why she ridiculed me," I said. "In a serious discussion she couldn't keep up. She never saw what I saw. But that wasn't my fault, you understand."

"I don't want to say too much. Only, Mitch, listen. It isn't that you're smart and Crystal isn't. It's just that...."

"What? Go on. Say it."

"I'm not sure I can get it to come out like it should. I think it's better if I stop right where I am."

I forced myself to stay the entire month, holding onto the chance of Crystal's appearance, even for a day or an afternoon, because she had often expressed to Florence how she loved the camp and the quiet relaxation of the mountains. Carl and I resumed our usual sessions at one or the other's picnic table. During a particularly listless hour when neither of us had much to say, I attempted to explain the digital camera and its countless features. He stopped me before I could tout the LCD.

"This is the only camera I've ever owned," he said, raising the old, German-made 35-millimeter, "and it's more than I need."

In recent years I'd noticed Carl had been taking fewer pictures. He continued to bring out the camera because it seemed he feared a great photographic moment would occur the first time he didn't. As for myself, I depressed the button at every opportunity. Wildflowers, a dead leaf, a deserted hornets' nest, an array of spider webs and the little psychopaths themselves waiting patiently on the cabin's picture window. Weathered boards rich in reddish tones on the backside of my neighbors' camp. I captured two heron spear-fishing at dawn in the shallows of the pond. I photographed Florence without her knowing, perhaps a half-dozen times, and snapped a couple of shots of Carl, alone and staring at nothing. During the final week the grandsons, both now in their late teens, appeared. The younger stayed overnight. He fished and provided a few artistic images of his silhouette with a motionless pond out front. After his departure, the handsome one drove in, girlfriend sitting close. They stayed only for the day and I got shots of them in the water and out. The young woman proved to be photogenic, and she liked having a lens train on her.

Returning home, I dumped the entire collection of photos onto the hard drive of my pc. It was Florence who captured my greatest attention with her composed, saintly countenance. Too saintly for what she revealed about herself. Would I tell a brilliant man he was such? Would I say to another person, man or woman, that I was of lesser intelligence? Would Crystal, I wondered.

Later that same day, I cropped the photo of my summer neighbors, taken as they'd sat across from me at the picnic table. While waiting on the printer, I wrote the following note that would accompany the blow-up: *"Dear Carl, unlike you, I didn't throw away the negatives. I haven't any. — Best, Mitch."*

That was the last time I communicated with them. A month later, Crystal got in touch and we put the cabin up for sale.

www.ingramcontent.com/pod-product-compliance
Lightning Source LLC
Chambersburg PA
CBHW060121260626
47160CB00005B/1961